ON THE ROAD . . .

Red Dorakeen has been traveling the Road as far back as he or anyone else can remember. A long, long time ago, he walked it as an old man—now, much younger, he's driving his beat-up blue Dodge pick-up, running guns to the Greeks fighting Persian invaders at ancient Marathon.

But someone has put out a contract on Red—filed legal notice of a series of ten attempts to murder him, under the laws that govern the Road. His hidden enemy has searched the past and future to recruit a band of assassins—human and otherwise, ranging from a lethal monk to a tyrannosaurus—to pursue Red wherever the Road might take him.

Roadmarks

Roger Zelazny

A Del Rey Book

BALLANTINE BOOKS • NEW YORK

Library of Congress Catalog Card Number: 79-2280

ISBN 0-345-25388-4

Manufactured in the United States of America

First Edition: October 1979

Paperback format
First Edition: August 1980
Third Printing: November 1981

Cover art by Darrell K. Sweet

To Ron Bounds,
Bobbie Armbruster,
Gary & Uschi Klüpfel,
with happy memories
of Oktoberfest

Two

"Pull over!" cried Leila.

Randy cut to the right immediately and braked the car. The sky pulsed its way to a pearly predawn.

"Back up along the shoulder."

He nodded and shifted into reverse.

"Those people? We could just walk back—"

"I want to look at them more closely before we get out."

"Okay," he said as they crept backward.

She turned and regarded the battered gray vehicle. There were two figures seated within it. Both seemed to be white-haired, but the light was still tricky. Both seemed to be watching her.

"In a moment, the door on the driver's side will open," she said softly.

The door on the driver's side opened.

"Now the other."

The other door opened.

"The old man was driving, the old woman a passenger . . ."

An old man and an old woman stepped out and moved forward, leaving the doors open behind them. They wore ragged wraparound garments held in place with sashes.

1

"Stop," she said. "Let's get out and go back and help them. Their distributor cap has come loose."

"A part of your vision?"

"No," she said.

She opened the door, got out and headed back. He did the same. His first impression, as he approached, was that the man was too old to be driving. Stoop-shouldered, he leaned against his car. His free hand trembled slightly; it was dry and spotted, clawlike. His face was heavily lined, his eyebrows as white as his hair. Then the eyes caught Randy and held him—green, almost flashing. There was an awareness there at which he would not have guessed from three meters farther back. Randy smiled at him, but the man showed no reaction.

Leila, in the meantime, had approached the old woman and was speaking with her in a language Randy did not recognize.

"If I could take a look under the hood," Randy suggested, "I might be of some help."

When the man did not respond, he repeated it in foretalk lingo. This drew no reaction either. The man seemed to be studying his face, his garments, his movements. Randy felt uncomfortable before that peculiar scrutiny. He cast Leila a look of appeal.

"It's all right," she said. "Go ahead and open the hood and fix it. They don't understand how it works. I'm explaining about fuel now."

As he bent to unfasten the latch, Randy saw Leila pass a large wad of money to the old woman. The man drew back as the hood rose several inches. When Randy had raised it to a full open position, he heard a brief exclamation from that direction.

Yes. The distributor cap had come loose. He fitted it back into place and clamped it there. Casting a quick glance over the rest of the engine, he saw nothing out of order.

"Would you care to try starting it now, sir?" he asked.

When he looked up, the man was smiling at him.

"I'm not sure you understand me, but I'd like to try starting the engine now," Randy said. Then, when the other did not move or reply, he said, "I'll do it."

Randy moved around the man, looked into the car. The key was still in the ignition. He slid inside and tried it. A moment later, the engine caught. He turned it off and climbed out again. He smiled back at the old man and nodded.

"There you are."

The man suddenly lunged forward and embraced him in a bear hug. He was surprisingly strong, and his breath came very hot.

"Name, your name, good man?" he said.

"Randy. I'm Randy—Dorakeen," he replied, extricating himself.

"Dorakeen. Good name," said the other.

Leila had circled the vehicle and now stood behind them. The old woman had followed her.

"They'll be okay," she said. "Come on. We must go now—to the last exit to Babylon."

She hissed something at the man, who nodded. She embraced the old woman for a long moment, then pulled herself away and started back toward the car. Randy followed quickly. When he glanced back, the couple had already entered their vehicle. He heard the engine turn over. Then the car pulled out onto the Road and was gone. At that moment, the sun came up and he noticed that Leila was crying. He looked the other way and had strange feelings.

One

Red Dorakeen was on a quiet section of the Road, straight and still as death and faintly sparkling. A pair of futuristic vehicles had passed him several hours earlier, moving at fantastic speeds, and he had later overtaken a coach-and-four and then a solitary horseman. He kept his blue Dodge pickup in the right-hand lane and maintained a steady 65 mph. He chewed his cigar and hummed.

The sky was a very pale blue with a heavy bright line running from east to west across it. There was no noticeable dust, and no insects splattered against the windshield.

He drove with the window down, his left hand clasping the top of the doorframe. He wore a faded baseball cap, its bill drawn low over his forehead; his head was tilted slightly back to accommodate it, his green eyes half-lidded in its shadow. His ruddy beard might have been slightly darker than his hair.

A tiny spot appeared far ahead. It grew rapidly, resolving into a battered black Volkswagen. As they passed, the other vehicle's horn began to sound. It drew off onto the shoulder of the Road and came to a halt.

Red glanced into his side mirror, hit his brakes

and drifted to his right. As he slowed, the sky began to pulse—blue, gray, blue, gray—its bright stripe vanishing with each fading stroke.

When he came to a complete stop, a clear evening hung about him. Crickets sounded somewhere in the distance, and a cool breeze passed. He opened the door and climbed down from the cab, yanking his ignition keys and pocketing them as he descended. He wore Levi's and combat boots, a brown ski vest over his khaki work shirt, and a wide belt with an elaborate buckle. He reversed his cap and paused to light his cigar before he turned and hiked back along the shoulder.

There was no way to cross the Road without risking almost certain destruction. For this reason, he moved to a spot directly across from the Volkswagen. As he did, the car's door opened and a short man with a small moustache emerged.

"Red!" he called. "Red? . . ."

"What is it, Adolph?" he hollered. "Still looking for the place where you won?"

"Listen, Red," said the other. "I didn't know whether to tell you this or not, because I couldn't make up my mind whether I hated you more than I felt I owed you. But then, I could not decide whether the information would be harmful or useful to you. So I guess it all balances out. I am going to tell you. I was way the hell down the Road earlier, and I saw it happen at the exit marked with the blue ziggurat—"

"The blue ziggurat?"

"The blue ziggurat. I saw you turn over going off there. I saw your truck burn."

Red Dorakeen was silent for several moments. Then he laughed.

"Death," he said, "will surely be puzzled if he passes me soon. He will say, 'What is this man doing in Themistocles' Athens when he has a date with me on the last exit to Babylon?' "

His great frame shook as he laughed again. Then he blew smoke and raised his right arm in a gesture of mock salute.

"But thanks," he said. "It may be a good thing for me to know."

He turned and started back toward his truck.

"One thing more," the other called after him.

He halted and turned his head.

"What's that?"

"You could have been a great man. Good-bye."

"*Auf wiedersehen.*"

Red mounted to the cab and started the engine. Soon the sky was blue again.

Two

As dawn worked its way above the still and shattered skyline, Strangulena stirred on her barge in the East River. Slowly, gently, she pushed back the fur that covered them, and brushed a strand of flaming hair from her brow. Her fingertips touched the more sensitive spots on her throat, shoulders and breasts, where the signs of her lover's ardor were already becoming visible. Smiling then, she flexed her fingers and turned slowly onto her left side.

Toba, as heavy and dark as the departing night, his cheek resting on his right palm, grinned at her.

"Gods! Don't you ever sleep?" she said.

"Not with a lady who has strangled over a hundred lovers once they'd dropped off beside her."

Her eyes narrowed.

"Then you knew! All along you knew! You led me on!"

"Thank God and amphetamine, yes!"

She smiled and stretched.

"You are very fortunate. Actually, I don't normally wait for them to drop off. I generally choose a certain moment and they come and go at the same time, so to speak. You were going to get it now only because I was distracted by architecture then. However . . ."

She reached out and manipulated the control unit. Silently, the barge began to move.

She turned onto her other side.

"Look how the light hits the Manhattan ruins! I just adore ruins!" She sat up suddenly and raised an oblong rectangle of carved and polished wood. She held it at arm's length and stared through it. "That group right there . . . Isn't that a fine composition?"

Toba raised himself and leaned forward, his chin brushing her left shoulder.

"It's—uh—interesting."

She held a small camera in her left hand, sighted through it, through the frame, leaned forward, leaned back, pressed a button.

"Got it."

She deposited the frame and the camera off to her right.

"I could spend my life viewing picturesque ruins. In fact, I do. Most of the time. They're always best from the water. Did you ever notice that?"

"Now that you mention it . . ."

"You were too good to be true, you know? Dressed in rags, poking through junk at the water's edge, unscrubbed and unlettered, a product of civilization's decay—just as I drifted by. You conned me. What are you? An archaeologist?"

"Well . . ."

". . . And you knew about me. Keep your right arm up like that, but raise your head."

She rolled over onto her stomach, raised her own right arm, and clasped his hand.

"All right, Mister Toba. Start pushing as if your life depended on it. Maybe it does."

"Hey now, lady—"

His arm began bending backward. He tightened his grip, strained. It halted for a few moments. He clamped his jaw, leaned left.

Suddenly he was slammed back, his arm pinned to the deck.

She smiled down at him.

"Want to try it with your left?"

"No, thanks. Look, I believe everything I've heard about you . . . You have—uh—exotic tastes and you're strong enough to satisfy them. I've got to admire anybody who gets what they want. This was the only way I knew to meet you, though. I've got a once-in-a-lifetime offer you can't afford to miss."

"Does it involve a good ruin?"

"You'd better believe it!" he said quickly.

". . . And a good man?"

"One of the best!"

She seized his hand and jerked him to his feet.

"Quick! Look at the sunlight on that broken tower!"

"Sure is something!"

"What's his name?"

"Dorakeen. Red Dorakeen."

"That sounds familiar . . ."

"He's been around a lot."

"Is he picturesque?"

"Need you ever ask?"

"I could use a new barge, with some ivory inlay work . . ."

"Say no more. Hey! Sunlight through what's left of that bridge!"

"Quick! The camera! —You're a very lucky man, Toba."

"Don't I know it!"

One

When he saw the tiny dot in the rearview mirror blossom and gleam, Red Dorakeen cursed softly.

"What is the matter?" came a husky voice from the dashboard.

"Huh? I didn't know I'd left you on."

His right hand moved toward the control knob, then dropped back.

"You didn't. I activated the circuit myself."

"How'd you manage that?"

"Remember the service job I won from you in that card game last month? There was sufficient credit remaining to have them install some extra circuits. I'd decided it was time to expand my horizons."

"You mean you've been eavesdropping on me for an entire month?"

"Yes. You talk to yourself a lot. It's fun."

"We'll have to do something about that."

"You could stop playing cards with me. —I repeat, what is the matter?"

"Police car. Coming up fast. May go right on by. May not, too."

"I'll bet I can knock him out. Want to fight?"

"Hell, no. Sit tight, Flowers. Certain things take time, that's all."

"I do not understand."

"I am in no hurry. If I fail, I try again. Or I try something else."

His eyes returned to the mirror. The shining, teardrop-shaped vehicle was large now in the passing lane and still gaining, though it seemed that it might have slowed.

"I still do not understand."

He struck a wooden match with his thumbnail and relit his cigar.

"I know. Don't worry about it—and stay out of any discussions that might arise."

"Acknowledged."

He glanced to the side. The vehicle had come abreast of him and was pacing him now. He sighed.

"Stop me or go on, damn you!" he muttered. "We're both too big to play games!"

As if in response, a siren wailed. A globe reared itself above the shining roof and began to blink like a hot eye.

Red turned the steering wheel and drew off onto the Road's shoulder. Again, the sky began to pulse, dark and light, darker and lighter. When the vehicle came to a complete halt, a morning sun hovered just above the horizon to his right, the grasses were pale with frost, birds were singing. The shining vehicle pulled off ahead of him. Both its doors opened and two gray-tunicked officers descended and moved in his direction. He turned off the ignition and sat perfectly still. He exhaled a large cloud of smoke.

The driver of the other vehicle came up beside his door. His companion moved toward the rear of the truck. The first man looked in. He smiled faintly.

"I'll be damned!" he said.

"Hi, Tony."

"Didn't know it was you, Red. Hope you're not up to anything too gross."

Red shrugged.

"Oh, a little of this, a little of that."

"Tony," came a voice from the rear. "You'd better take a look at this."

"Uh . . . I'll have to ask you to step down, Red."

"Sure."

He opened the door and climbed out.

"What is it?" Tony asked, moving back.

"Look."

He had undone a corner of the tarp and raised it. He now proceeded to unfasten it further.

"I recognize those! They're C Twenty rifles, called M-1s."

"Yeah, I know. See what's back here? Browning Automatic Rifles. And this is a case of hand grenades. Lots of ammo, too."

Tony sighed, turned.

"Don't tell me. Let me guess," he said. "I know right where you are going. You still believe the Greeks should win the Battle of Marathon and you want to give them a hand."

Red grimaced.

"What makes you guess that?"

"You've been caught at it twice before."

"And you just pulled me over—part of a random sampling?"

"That's right."

"You trying to say that no one tipped you off?"

The officer hesitated and glanced away.

"That's right."

Red grinned around the cigar.

"Okay. You've got me with the goods. What are you going to do?"

"The first thing we are going to do is confiscate the stuff. You can give us a hand loading them into our van."

"Do I get a receipt?"

"Damn it, Red! Don't you know the seriousness of what you're doing?"

"Yep."

"Admitted, nothing will happen to us if you can pull it off. You will create another branch in the Road, though. Or another exit."

"What's wrong with that—really?"

"Who knows who might start traveling it from that point."

"A lot of weird fish travel it already, Tony. Look at us."

"But you're a devil we know. Everybody knows you. Why do you want that other goddamned branch anyway?"

"Because it was that way once before, but that sideroad is now blocked. I am trying to re-create a set of circumstances."

"I don't remember it."

"You're young, Tony."

"I don't understand you, Red. Come on, give me a hand with these weapons."

"Okay."

They began transferring the pieces.

"You know you have to stop this sort of thing."

"I know that watching for it is a part of your job, yes."

"But you don't give a damn. Supposing you were to open the route to some really rotten place, full of dangerous, vicious creatures with the ability to move along the Road? We'd all be in trouble then. Why not lay off this business?"

"I'm looking for something I haven't been able to find any other way."

"Mind telling me what?"

"Yes, I do. It's personal."

"You'd foul up the whole traffic pattern just for some selfish little whim?"

"Yep."

"Don't know why I asked. I've known you for about forty years. What's that come to for you?"

"Five or six years. Thirty, maybe. I don't know. You doing a lot of office work in between?"

"Too much."

"Probably where you got those notions about new branches."

"As a matter of fact, I did pick up a lot of the theory, and it is more complicated than you probably think."

"Hogwash! It was that way once, it can be that way again."

"Have it your way, but we won't have you messing around like this."

"People do it every day. Why else would they travel the Road? Everywhere they go, they alter the branches some way or other."

Tony's teeth clicked.

"I know, and that's frightening enough. This whole thing ought to be better controlled, check points set up—"

"But the Road has always been here, and those of us w'o can travel it always have. The world goes on, the Road goes on—from creation to destruction, amen, for all you know. What's your point?"

"I've known you for forty years—or thirty, or five or six. You haven't changed. I can't talk to you. —Okay. We can't control most of the traffic, we can't stop the minor changes. We can look out for big things, though, and we do. You're always involved with the big ones. I'm trying to be nice and let you go with another warning."

"That's all you can do, and you know it. You can't prove where I was headed with this equipment. You can confiscate, you can lecture, you can make things rough for me for a while. But it won't last—and you know as well as I do that you are handing me another line. This isn't policy or guarding the peace or anything like that. You are harassing me, personally, for a particular reason. Someone's down on me and I'd like to know who, and why."

Tony reddened. His partner passed them with a carton of grenades.

"You're getting paranoid, Red," he finally said.

"Uh-uh. Care to give me a hint?" His eyes were fixed on the other's as he struck a match on an ammo box and relit his cigar. "Who could it be?"

Tony glanced at his partner, then, "Come on. Let's get the rest of this stuff loaded," he said.

It took another ten minutes to transfer the balance of the arms. When this had been done, Red was permitted to enter his truck.

"Okay. Consider yourself warned," Tony said.

Red nodded.

"...And be careful."

Red nodded again, more slowly.

"Thanks."

He watched them mount their shining vehicle and speed off.

"What was that all about?"

"He just did me a favor, Flowers. He came looking, to let me know we're in trouble."

"What kind?"

"I'll have to think about it. Where's the nearest rest stop?"

"Not too far ahead."

"You drive."

"Okay."

The truck jerked into motion.

Two

The Marquis de Sade followed Sundoc into the enormous building.

"I appreciate this considerably," he said, "and I'd appreciate your not mentioning it to Chadwick, because he thinks I'm reading a stack of abominable manuscripts. Ever since Baron Cuvier's speculations, I have wondered, I have wished. But I never thought that I would actually get to see one."

Sundoc chuckled and led him into the huge laboratory.

"I can appreciate that. Don't worry. I like to show off my work."

They approached the great pit in the center of the hall, coming up to the railing that surrounded it.

Sundoc gestured with his right hand and the area below was flooded with light.

It stood like an enormous statue, like an unusually well-fashioned prop for a Grade B movie, like a suddenly materialized neurosis . . .

And then it moved. It shuffled its feet and lowered its head away from the light. A strip of gleaming metal was revealed at the back of its head, and another farther down along its spine.

"Ugly as they come," said Sundoc.

The marquis shook his head.

"God's dentures! It's beautiful!" he said softly. "Tell me again what it is called."

"*Tyrannosaurus rex.*"

"Fitting. Yes, so fitting! It's lovely!"

He stood unmoving for over a minute. Then he asked, "How did you obtain this wonderful beast? I was given to believe that they only existed in the extremely distant past."

"True. It took a fusion-powered vessel flying above the Road at a very good clip for a very long while to get back that far."

"Yet the Road does extend back to those days . . . Amazing! And how did you transport something of that size, that power?"

"Didn't. The team I sent narcotized one and brought a tissue sample to a period about fifteen years back. This specimen was cloned from that sample—that is to say, he is an artificially cultivated twin of the original."

"Beautiful, oh beautiful! I don't understand, but it does not make a bit of difference—adds to the charm, the mystery, in fact. Now, tell me of your control over it."

"You see those metallic plates on its head and back?"

"Yes."

"They are implant grids. A great number of tiny electrodes extend down from them into the creature's nervous system. A moment . . ."

He walked away, crossing to a workstand from which he obtained a small rectangular box and a silver basket. He returned with these and displayed them.

"This," he said, indicating the box, "is a computer—"

"A thinking machine?"

"Oh, someone has been briefing you. Well, sort of. This one is also a broadcast unit."

He threw a switch. A tiny light came on behind a dial. There was no sound.

"You can make it do whatever you want—with that?"

"Better than that."

He fitted the basket over his head, adjusted its band. "Far better," he said, "for there is feedback."

The reptile raised its head, turned it to regard them. ". . . I see two men looking down at me. One is wearing something shiny on his head. I am going to wave to them—my right forelimb."

Grotesquely, ludicrously, the relatively tiny appendage began a waving movement.

". . . And now I will shout my greeting!"

A bellow that rattled equipment on distant tables, that seemed to shake the very building, rolled about them.

"I must! I must!" cried the marquis. "Let me try! Please let me try it!"

Sundoc grinned and removed the headgear.

"Sure. It's easy. I'll show you how to put it on . . ."

For several minutes, the marquis marched the monster about its pit, waving its tail, stamping its feet.

"I really can see through its eyes!"

"That's the feedback part I was telling you about."

"My— Its strength must be phenomenal!"

"Oh, it is."

Several additional minutes passed, then, "I am really loath to surrender this sensation," he observed, "but I suppose I must. How do you turn it off?"

"Here, I'll show you."

He removed the headpiece, switched off the control unit.

"I have never known such a sensation of power," said the marquis. "Why— There would be the invincible weapon, the perfect assassin. Why do you not use it to kill that Dorakeen fellow and claim the bounty your master is offering?"

Sundoc laughed.

"Can you see it lumbering along the Road toward some guessed-at rendezvous, to step on his enemy? No, transportation would be an insuperable problem, even if we did know exactly where to deliver the beast. I never intended to use it in any such fashion. Far too cumbersome."

"True, true—when you put it that way. It was the imagery that took hold of me—the reptilian avenger swooping down upon its prey . . . The sensations of controlling it the while . . ."

"Um. I suppose so."

". . . Whereas it actually represents a noble enterprise for the advancement of science."

"Hardly. All of the techniques employed here are quite venerable. The control of that monster represents no gain for science. Whatever information may be obtained concerning the beast itself could as easily be gained simply by studying it in an untampered condition. No, what you see down there is the fulfillment of a whim—which is why I consented so readily to showing it off. I had always had a desire to do this for the pure fun of it. That's all. It is an end in itself. There is no special use for the beast. Oh, my assistants will study its physiology and publish their findings. Might as well take advantage of its presence that way. After a long and rewarding career, I can afford to indulge myself in this fashion. So why not?"

"We are closer together in some matters than I would have believed."

"Because I admit to an expensive indulgence?"

The marquis shook his head.

"Because you enjoy the feeling of such a peculiar power."

Sundoc moved his hand and darkened the pit. He drew back from the railing and turned away.

"All right," he said. "You have a point." He replaced the gear on the workbench as they moved away. "You'd best get back to those manuscripts now."

"Ouch," said the marquis. "From Olympus to Tartarus in only a few blocks."

Sundoc smiled.

"It eats a lot too," he said. "But it's worth it."

One

He entered the graveled lot and headed toward a group of hewn-log buildings before which stood rows of pumps for various fuels.

"How's the gas?" Red inquired.

"Half full, with a full auxiliary."

"Park, over by those trees."

He came to a halt beneath a large oak tree. The sun had already settled far into the west.

"We're around C Sixteen, aren't we?"

"Yes. Were you planning on getting off here?"

"No. I was just thinking: I once knew a guy from this period. Had to take the English cutoff, up a piece . . ."

"You want to park and go visit him?"

"No. He's—elsewhere. And I'm hungry. Come keep me company."

He withdrew a copy of *Flowers of Evil* from beneath the dashboard.

"Where did he go?" came the voice from the book.

"Who?"

"Your friend."

"Oh. Far. Yes, he went far." Red chuckled.

He opened the door and stepped outside. There was

a chill in the air. He moved quickly in the direction of the buildings.

The dining room was shadowy, its chandelier as yet unlit. The tables were of wood and uncovered, as was the floor. A log fire crackled in an open hearth at the room's far end. The only windows were in the front wall.

He glanced at the diners. Two couples were seated before the big window. Young-looking. From their garb and their speech, he placed them as late C Twenty-one. The garments of the delicate-looking man at the table to his right indicated late Victorian England as his place of origin. Seated with his back to the nearer wall was a dark-haired man wearing black trousers and boots, and a white shirt. He was eating chicken and drinking beer. A dark leather jacket hung over the back of his chair. Too basic. Red could not place him.

He moved to the farthest table, turned it, and sat with his back to the corner. He placed *Flowers of Evil* on the boards before him, opening the volume at random.

" '*Pour l'enfant, amoureux de cartes et d'estampes, l'univers est égal à son vaste appétit,*' " came the tiny voice.

He quickly raised the book to cover his face.

"True," he replied in a whisper.

"Yet you want more, don't you?"

"Just my own little corner."

"And where might that be?"

"Damned if I know."

"I've never quite understood why you do the things—"

A tall, white-haired waiter came up beside the table.

"Your order— Red!"

He looked up, stared a moment.

"Johnson? . . ."

"Yes. Good Lord! It's been years!"

"Has it? You used to work farther down the Road, didn't you?"

"Yes. But I like it better up here."

"I'm glad you found a good spot. Say, that guy's chicken looks good." Red nodded toward the dark-haired man. "So does his beer. I'll have the same. Who is he, anyway?"

"Never saw him before."

"All right. Bring the beer now."

"Okay."

He withdrew a fresh cigar from a concealed pocket, examined it.

Johnson paused, regarding him.

"Are you going to do the trick?"

"What trick?"

"I once saw you light your cigar with a coal you plucked from the fire. You weren't burned."

"Go on!"

"Don't you remember? It was some years ago . . . Unless you are going to learn it later. You *did* look older then. Anyway, it was about half a C down the Road."

Red shook his head.

"Some childish trick. I'll none of it now. Let's have the brew and the bird."

Johnson nodded and departed.

By the time Red had finished eating, the dining room had filled. Lights had been lit and the background noise had grown louder. He hailed Johnson, paid his tab and rose.

Outside, the night had become colder. He stepped down into the lot and turned left, heading toward his truck.

"Quiet," came the small word from the book he bore.

"Yes. I—"

The impact staggered him just as he saw the flash from the muzzle and heard the weapon's report.

Not pausing to assess the damage, he threw himself

to the side, his right arm whipping across his body. There came a second shot, but he felt nothing. With a snapping movement, he hurled *Flowers of Evil* at the shadowy gunman, then broke into a run toward his vehicle.

He tore around the front of the truck to the passenger side, pulled the door open, and threw himself flat within. As he groped beneath the seat for the .45 he kept there, he heard footfalls on the gravel on the other side. A voice from a greater distance on that side called out, "Hold it, mithter! You're covered!" There followed a gunshot and a soft curse, just as his fingers wrapped around the butt of the heavy revolver. He fired once, up and out through the window on the driver's side— a moment's insurance. Then he backed out and crouched.

Sounds were now coming from the building, as though the front door had been flung open and numerous loud conversations were in progress. There were several shouted inquiries. No one seemed to be approaching, however.

He stayed low and moved to the rear of the truck. Glancing behind him, he dropped to all fours, peered beyond the tailgate, looked around the bumper. Nothing. No one in sight . . .

He listened for a telltale footfall, heard none. He moved around to the rear, crawled toward the left side.

"He'th in front, heading right," came a sharp whisper.

He heard a sound from the front then, a hasty foot on gravel . . .

He tossed a rock behind him, to the right of the truck. No response. He waited.

Then, "Looks like a stalemate," he called out in foretalk lingo. "Want to discuss it?"

No reply.

"Any special reason for wanting to shoot me?" he tried.

Again, silence.

He rounded the left rear corner of the vehicle and started forward, rising into a low crouch, placing each foot carefully, easing his weight onto it.

"Thtop! He'th backed off into the treeth. Mutht be covering the front."

He transferred the weapon to his left hand and slid his right arm in through the open window. He jerked on the headlight switch and threw himself flat, to peer around the left front tire. A shot from the trees passed through the windshield on the driver's side.

From where he had fallen, Red saw the partial silhouette of the gunman drawing back for cover. He fired at it. The figure jerked and fell heavily against the tree trunk. He fired again as it began to slide downward, a pistol slipping from its fingers. The figure spun backward, struck the ground and lay still.

Red rose and advanced, covering the fallen man.

. . . Black trousers, a black jacket with a leaking hole drilled through its lower right quadrant. It was the man he had seen in the dining room earlier, with his back to the wall. Red put an arm about his shoulders, supported his head, raised him.

Pinkish bubbles had formed about the man's lips. He gasped as he was raised. His eyes flickered open.

"Why?" Red asked. "Why were you trying to shoot me?"

The man smiled weakly.

"I'd rather leave you—with something to think about," he said.

"It won't do *you* any good," Red said.

"Nothing will," replied the other. "So the devil with you!"

Red slapped him across the mouth, smearing the bloody spittle. He heard a gasp of protest from behind him as he did. A crowd was forming.

"Talk, you son of a bitch! Or I'll make it harder than it's going to be!"

He jabbed him in the upper abdomen with stiff fingers, near the wound.

"Here! Stop that!" said a voice from behind him.

"Talk!"

But the man followed a sharp gasp with a long sigh and stopped breathing. Red began hammering at his chest beneath the sternum.

"Come back, you miserable bastard!"

He felt a hand on his shoulder and shook it off. The gunman was not responding. He let him fall and began going through his pockets.

"I don't think you should be doing that," came another voice from behind.

Finding nothing of interest, Red rose.

"What car was this guy driving?" he asked.

Silence, then murmurs. Finally, "He was a hitch-hiker," the Victorian gentleman stated.

Red turned. The man was staring at the body, smiling faintly.

"How do you know that?" Red asked.

The man withdrew a silk handkerchief, unfolded it, touched it several times to his brow.

"I saw him being dropped off here earlier," he replied.

"From what sort of vehicle?"

"Black, C Twenty, a Cadillac."

"Did you get a look at anyone else in the car?"

The man looked back at the body, licked his lips, smiled again.

"No."

Johnson came up with a piece of sailcloth and covered the body. He picked up the fallen pistol and stuck it behind his belt. Rising, he placed a hand on Red's shoulder.

"I'm setting out a bleeper," he said, "but there's no telling how long it will take to call us a cop. You should stay to give a report, you know."

"Yeah, I'll wait."

"Let's get back then. I'll get you a room and a drink."

"Okay. Just a minute."

Red returned to the parking area and retrieved his book.

"That bullet damaged my thpeaker," came its sibilant voice.

"I know. I'll get you a new one, the best they make. Thanks for stopping it. And thanks for distracting him."

"I hope it wath worth it. Why wath he thooting at you?"

"I don't know, Flowers. I've got the impression that he was what is known in some places as a hit man. Possibly Syndicate. If so, there is no connection between his employers and myself that I can think of. I just don't know."

He slipped the volume into his pocket, then followed Johnson back inside.

Two

Randy spotted the blue pickup pulling out, and nosed into the parking place.

"This is the place?" he said, looking toward Spiro's.

Leila nodded, not looking up from her reading of *Leaves of Grass*.

"It was, at the time I was seeing, back in Africa," she said. "Now that we're in real time here, I don't know how close to synch it is."

"Translate."

"He might not have arrived yet, or he might already have departed."

Randy pulled on the emergency brake.

"Wait here and I'll go check," she said, opening the door, tossing the book onto the rear seat, and stepping out.

"Okay."

"Randy?"

"Yeah, Leaves?"

"She's a very vital woman, isn't she?"

"I'd say so."

"Is she attractive?"

"Yes."

"Domineering, though."

"She knows how to go about what we're doing. I don't."

"True, true ... Who's that?"

An old man, a crusader's cross on his dirty tunic, shuffled up, humming to himself. He produced a grimy rag from his sash and began wiping the headlights, the windshield. He spat on a splattered butterfly, scraped it off with his thumbnail, ran the rag across it. Finally he came up on Randy's side, smiled and nodded.

"Nice day," he said.

"It is."

Randy fished around in his pocket, found a quarter, passed it to him. The man palmed it and nodded again.

"Thank you, sir."

"You look like a—crusader."

"Am. Or was," he said in foretalk lingo. "Took a wrong turn somewhere and never found my way back. Can't hold it against a man if he gets lost, can you? Besides, someone told me the Crusade's over and we won. Then another traveler told me it's over and we lost. Either way, it'd be kind of silly to go on—and I like it here. One of these days a bishop'll drive up in his Cadillac and I'll get him to release me from my vow. In the meantime, they let me sleep around back, and the cook feeds me." He winked. "And I make enough out here to get pickled every night in the tap-room. Softest life I've ever had. No sense in looking for a fight when the war's over, is there?"

Randy shook his head.

"You wouldn't know for sure, would you?"

"Know what?"

"Who won."

"The Crusades?"

The other nodded.

Randy rubbed his nose.

"Well . . . According to my history books, there were four big ones and a number of so-so ones. As to who won, that's not an easy question to answer—"

"That many!"

"Yeah. Sometimes you guys came off ahead and sometimes the other guys did. There were all sorts of reversals and intrigues. Betrayals . . . A lot of good cultural transmission went on. It opened the way for restoring Greek philosophy to the West. It—"

"The hell with all that, lad! In your day, who has the Holy Land, them or us?"

"Them, mostly—"

". . . And what about our lands? Have we got them or do they?"

"We do, but—"

The old soldier chuckled.

"Then nobody won."

"It's not that cut-and-dried. Nobody really lost, either. You've got to look at the larger picture. You see—"

"Balls! It's all right for you to read about larger pictures, son. I don't feel like going back and getting a scimitar up the bunghole for your larger picture, though. Louis can keep his Crusade. I feel a lot better about wiping the glass in your Devil's chariot and staying soused right here, now that I know nobody won."

"Of course I see your point, even if you do lack a sense of history about it. But it's not right to say—"

"Damn right! And if you're lucky, someone from up the Road will come along and do you the same favor one day. Tell him about history if he does." He flipped the quarter into the air and caught it. "Keep the faith, kid." He turned and limped away.

Randy nodded and located one of Leila's cigars.

"Interesting . . ." he muttered.

On the seat in back, Leaves began to hum softly. Then, "You are unhappy about something?" she asked.

"Perhaps. I don't know. What makes you ask?"

"I have been observing your heartbeat, your metabolism, your blood pressure, your breathing. Everything seems elevated. That's all."

"Then I can't hide much from you, can I? I was

thinking how the passions of a Crusade—or a broken love affair—are but moments in geological time."

"True. But since you are not a rock or a glacier, what difference does that make?" Then, "You have terminated such a relationship recently?"

"I guess that's one way of putting it, yes."

"Sad, perhaps. Or not, as the case may be. You—"

"Not," he said. "Not really. It was something not meant to go on. Yet there is a feeling of loss . . . Why am I telling you this?"

"Everyone finds someone to tell things to. At a time like this you must be careful. Following a loss, one often seeks to fill that place with something new. One chooses in haste, rather than wisely. One—"

"Here comes Leila now," Randy said.

"Oh."

There was silence.

Randy drew on the cigar. He considered the clouds reflected in the hood. He regarded the bewildering array of vehicles drawn up about him, like some display in a museum of transportation.

"I do not detect her approach," Leaves said after a time.

"Sorry. I was mistaken."

There came a burst of static. Then, "Sorry, Randy. I wasn't trying to intrude."

"That's all right."

"It's just that I wanted to—"

"She *is* coming now."

"Okay. I just— Never mind."

Leila jerked the door open, climbed in and slammed it. She reached over and removed the cigar from between his fingers. She took a long drag on it and slumped in the seat.

"I take it you didn't—" he began.

"Shh! We're practically bumper to bumper now. Only there was no forwarding address. I have to look again."

He watched as her gaze drifted through the smoke. Her face grew expressionless for a time, then emotions flickered across it too rapidly for him to classify.

"Start the engine! Drive!" she ordered.

"Where?"

"Down the Road. I'll know the turnoff when it happens. Let's go!"

He backed out of the parking place, swung toward the exit.

"I'm beginning to understand ..."

"What?" he asked.

"What we are," she said, passing him the cigar.

He pressed the accelerator and sped.

One

Red rolled out of bed, grabbed for his vest.

"Hey! Hell of a smoke-detector you are!"

"That part of me mutht have been damaged altho."

He withdrew a small, flat flashlight from the garment's pocket as he slipped it on. He sent its beam about the room, but there was no smoke. Rising, he moved to the door. He halted there and sniffed.

"Maybe you'd better not . . ."

Opening the door, he stepped out into the hall, sniffed again and moved to his left.

There! The next room!

He ran to the door, pounded on it, tried the knob. It was locked.

"Wake up!"

Stepping back, he kicked hard, next to the lock. The door flew open. Smoke rolled by him. He rushed in to behold a burning bed, a smiling woman still apparently asleep within it.

Stooping, he raised her from the flames and bore her across the room. He dumped her onto the floor, her clothing still smoldering, and returned to beat at the bed with a rug.

"Hey!" the woman called out.

"Shut up," he said. "I'm busy."

The woman rose to her feet, her clothing still afire. She ignored this for the better part of a minute and watched him assail the flames. Then, as the front of her garment flared, she glanced down at it. With a casual movement, she unfastened a tie behind her neck and let it fall to the floor. Stepping out of its circle of fire, she advanced.

"What are you doing here?" she asked.

"Trying to put out your goddamned fire! What were you doing, smoking in bed?"

"Yes," she replied. "Drinking too."

She knelt and reached beneath the bed. She retrieved a bottle.

"Let it burn," she said. "Have a drink. We'll watch it."

"Leila, stay out of my way!"

"Sure, Reyd. Anything you say."

She withdrew, seated herself in a large chair, looked about, rose again, crossed to the dresser, applied a candle that burned there to the wick of an oil lamp and picked up a goblet. She returned to the chair.

There were rapid footsteps in the hall. They slowed, stopped.

"How bad is it?" came Johnson's voice, followed by a cough.

"Just the bed," Red replied. "I've got it under control now."

"You can throw the mattress out the window when you're able to handle it. There's just gravel down there."

"Okay. I will."

"Room seventeen is empty, Miss Leila. You can have that one."

"Thanks, but I like it here."

Red moved to the window, unfastened the shutters, swung them back. Returning to the bed, he rolled the mattress, gathered it in his arms and bore it to the star-filled square, where he pushed it through.

"I'll have a new bed and mattress sent up," Johnson said.

"And another bottle."

Johnson, who had stepped inside, backed out into the hall, still coughing.

"Very well. I don't see how you people can breathe in there."

Red stared out the window. Leila opened her bottle. Johnson's footsteps retreated down the hall.

"Care for a drink, Reyd?"

"Okay."

He turned and walked to her. She handed him the goblet.

"Your health," he said, and sipped it.

She snorted and took a drink from the bottle.

"Here, that isn't ladylike," he said. "I'll trade you."

She chuckled.

"Never mind. I've the better part of the deal. —Your health. How is it, anyway?"

"The booze or my health?"

"Either one."

"I've had better and I've had worse. Either one. What are you doing here, Leila?"

She shrugged.

"Drinking. Turning a few tricks. What are you doing? Still racing up and down the Road, looking for an unmarked turnoff—or trying to open one?"

"More or less. For a long while I thought perhaps you had found the way and taken it. To find you here is—how shall I say it?—disillusioning."

"I've a way of producing that effect," she said, "haven't I?"

He withdrew a cigar from his vest, crossed to the candle, lit it.

"Got another of those on you?"

"Yeah."

He passed her the cigar, lit a second for himself.

"Why are you doing it?" he asked.

The smoke spiraled above her head.

"Doing what?"

"Doing nothing," he said. "Wasting your time here when you could be looking."

"Since you ask," she said, taking another drink, "I will tell you. I have been up and down that damned Road from the Neolithic to C Thirty. I have followed every sideroad, footpath and rabbit run along the way. I am known in a thousand lands by different names. Yet in none of them have I found what I sought, what we seek."

"You have never been close? You have never felt the presence?"

She shuddered.

"I have felt presences—some of them very similar, some of them quite unforgettable—none of them right. No. I can only conclude that the place I once sought no longer exists."

"Everything exists somewhere."

"Then you can't get there from here."

"I can't believe that."

"Then tell me this: is it worth it? Is it worth wasting your life looking when you can have your choice of times and places, go anywhere, do anything you want?"

"Like turning tricks and drinking yourself unconscious? Like setting fire to the bed?"

She blew a smoke ring.

"I have been doing nothing—as you said—for almost a year. It gets easier every day. And the results are the same. I have used up my energies. I am by nature quite indolent. It is pleasant to stop, to resign a fruitless enterprise. Why don't *you* join me? You have nothing to show for all your efforts. We could at least console one another."

"It is not my nature," he said, just as servants arrived with new bed, bedding and bottle.

They smoked in silence and watched the men work. When they had gone, she said, "Having a lot of money and sleeping much of the time are the best things in life."

"I am also interested in the things in between," he said.

"And what has it gotten you?" she asked, standing. "Marked for death, that's all."

She moved to the window and looked out.

"What do you mean?" he finally asked.

"Nothing."

"It sounded like something to me. Come on, what did you see?"

"I didn't say I saw anything." She turned toward him. "We've got a new bed. Let's try it."

"Don't try to distract me. I know you've got more of the Sight than I have. Let's have it."

She leaned back against the sill and took a long drink.

"And get away from that window. You might fall out."

"Always the big brother," she said, but she moved away and went to sit on the bed.

She placed the bottle on the floor and began drawing on her cigar, producing great clouds of smoke into which her gaze wandered.

"Seeing . . ." she said, then lapsed into silence.

"Seeing," Red repeated.

"You move in a fog. It thickens as you head toward death. And you desire it! I saw ten dark birds pursue you," she said, her voice dropping to a lower register, "and now there are nine . . ."

"Black decade!" he whispered. Then, "Who called it?"

"Big," she said. "A big, heavy man . . . And a poet . . . Yes, he is a poet. Why, of course!"

"Chadwick."

"Fat Chadwick," she agreed.

She blew the smoke away and reached for the bottle.

"Why, when and how?" Red asked.

"What do you want for one lousy vision? That's it."

"Chadwick," he repeated, then drained his goblet. "It does make a sort of sense. Many men have had the motive, but few others have had the means." Then, "Tony must have known something," he decided. "So he's gotten to them, too . . . That means I can't count on anything from the cops. But . . . Who can? It's official, then."

He rose, retrieved the bottle and poured some more wine into the goblet.

"What are you going to do?" she asked.

He took a sip.

"Keep going," he said.

She nodded.

"All right. I'll go with you. You'll need my help."

"Nope. Not now. Thanks."

She picked up the bottle and threw it out the window. Her green eyes flashed.

"Don't be noble. I'm still one of the toughest things you ever met. You know I can help you."

"Any other time, and you know how happy I'd be. Not when a black decade's been declared, though. Hell, one of us has to live, if only to avenge the other."

She sprawled suddenly on the bed.

"You'd love that, wouldn't you? And you'd love it to be me . . . Everything has just caught up with me," she said. "I must sleep. I can't force you, but neither do I accept your answer. Do as you would, Reyd, for I will certainly do the same. Good night."

"I want you to be reasonable about this!"

She began to snore.

He finished his drink, put out the lights and left the goblet on the dresser. He closed the door behind him and returned to his own room, where he began to dress.

"Are we burning?"

"No, Flowers. We're leaving."

"What'th wrong?"

"Got to get out of here quick."

"Have you given your report to the polithe, about latht night?"

"Hell, the next report may be about me if we don't move now. That guy I shot last night was no crazy. I'm under black decade."

"What'th that?"

He drew on his boots and began lacing them.

"Vendetta is what I call it. My enemy gets ten shots at me without interference. If they all miss, he's supposed to quit. It's kind of a game. Last night's was the first."

"Can't you hit back?"

"Sure. If I knew where to look. In the meantime, I'd better run. The Road is long. The game can take a lifetime. Always does, in fact, one way or the other."

"The cops won't do anything?"

"Nope. Not when it's official. The Games Board has jurisdiction then. And even if they wanted to, there aren't that many police—and most of them are from around C Twenty-three to Twenty-five, anyway. Too civilized, and not much good this far back."

"Tho go up the Road to where they're thtronger, and look for thome criminal violation in the game."

"No, my enemy lives up that way, and he probably has them in his pocket. I think that's what Tony was trying to tell me. Besides, their function is mainly traffic control. No, we're running back."

"You know who'th behind it?"

"Yeah, an old buddy of mine. We used to be partners. C'mon."

"But aren't you—"

"Sh! We're sneaking out."

"Without paying?"

"Just like the old days."

"I wathn't with you then."

"It's all right. I haven't changed much."

He closed the door quietly behind him and headed for the back stairs.

"Red?"

"Shh!"

"Thh, hell! How did they know you were going to thtop here? It wath a thpur-of-the-moment dethithion."

"I've been wondering about that myself," he whispered.

"—Unleth thomeone knowth where you latht fueled and hath calculated a great number of pothible thtops where you'd be likely to take on more."

"And covered all of them? Come on!"

"Jutht the probable oneth. Could thith Thadwick guy afford it?"

"Well, yes . . ."

"He'd have to thpend ath much or more hunting you down if you got wind of it and ethcaped the firtht guy, wouldn't he?"

"Yes, you're right. But now I think of it, he knows me awfully well. If he'd arranged for that confiscation of my load just where it occurred, he might have guessed I'd pulled in at the next stop to think things over."

"Maybe. You willing to take the thanthe?"

"What chance? That there's someone at the next stop, and the next, and the next?"

"Could be, couldn't it?"

"Yeah, you're right. I was too busy just now thinking of something more immediate. Like, that fellow who was supposed to take me out not being wherever he was to be picked up after the job was done. It must have been earlier this evening. When they learned I'd killed him and was still here, what do you figure they did?"

"Hard to thay."

"Could they be out there right now, waiting?"

"It doeth theem pothible, doethn't it? Could they be covering thith back door?"

"Perhaps. That's why we're going to look first, then make a dash for the trees. I think it's more likely, though, that they'd be watching the pickup, either from the trees or from another vehicle. Therefore, we'll work our way around through the woods."

He reached the door, cursed when he discovered it to be heavy and windowless, eased it open a crack, looked out. Farther, then . . .

"Nothing," he said. "No talking now till this is all over—unless it's a warning. I wish I'd remembered the earplug lead."

"You'll ficth my thpeaker thoon?"

"There's a place up the Road that can probably do it while I'm getting a new windshield. Don't worry."

He swung the door open and dashed toward the shelter of the trees, about fifteen meters distant. When he reached them, he swung around the nearest and crouched in the shadows at its base. He remained motionless for several moments, breathing through his opened mouth.

Nothing. No shots, shouts or sounds of movement. He crawled back into the stand of trees, his fingertips brushing the way before him. Finally, he turned to his right and made his way around the rear of the hostel, still crawling. Leila's room remained dark. He could smell the burnt mattress ticking.

He advanced until he had a full view of the parking lot. No additional vehicles seemed present in the light of the quarter-moon and a scattering of stars. He remained within the wood, however, heading toward the point where his attacker had fallen.

When he reached the spot, he discovered that the covered body still lay there, its shroud weighted down with stones. He crouched beside it, pistol in hand, and regarded his truck. Five minutes passed. Ten . . .

He advanced. He circled the truck, inspecting it, then entered on the driver's side. He placed his book in a slot beneath the dashboard, then inserted his ignition key.

"Thtop! Don't turn the key!"

"Why not?"

"I am trickling a minimal charge through the thythtem. There ith rethithtanth that doethn't belong."

"A bomb?"

"Perhapth."

Cursing, Red stepped out and opened the hood. He produced his flashlight and began an inspection. After a time, he slammed the hood and climbed back in, still cursing.

"Wath it a bomb?"

"Yes."

He started the engine.

"What did you do with it?"

"Chucked it back into the woods."

He put the truck into gear, backed up, turned and headed out of the lot, stopping only to top off the tank.

Two

He had left his vehicle at a roadstop several days distant, yet worlds away. He was excessively tall and thin, with a great shock of dark hair above his high forehead, and he seemed garishly garbed for the mountains of Abyssinia. He wore purple khaki trousers and a purple shirt; even his boots and belt were of dyed purple leather; ditto his large backpack. Several amethyst rings adorned his abnormally long fingers. As he hiked along the rocky trail, apparently oblivious to the chill wind, it seemed he could almost be a young Romantic poet off on a *Wanderjahr*, save that the nineteenth century was eight hundred years in the future. Hollow eyes burning in his near-emaciated face, he searched for obscure landmarks and found them. He had not rested the entire day, even taking his rations as he walked. Now, though, he paused, for two distant peaks had finally come into line and the end of his journey was in sight.

Several hundred meters ahead, the trail widened, forming a large, flat bank which ran backward into a recess in the mountainside. He moved again, heading in that direction. When he reached the level area, he advanced into the recess. Walls of rock towered on either hand as he moved through the defile.

At length, passing through a wooden gate, he emerged into a small valley. Cows munched the grasses within it. There was a pool at its farther end. Nearer, a corral stood beside one of several cave mouths. Seated before that entranceway was a short, baldheaded black man. He was enormously fat, and his thick fingers caressed the turning clay on a treadle-operated potter's wheel.

He looked up, regarding the stranger who greeted him in Arabic.

". . . And peace be with you," he replied in that language. "Come and refresh yourself."

The purple-clad stranger approached.

"Thank you."

He dropped his pack and squatted across from the potter.

"My name is John," he said.

". . . And I am Mondamay, the potter. Excuse me. I am not being rude, but I cannot desert the pot at this point. It will take me several more minutes to be assured it will grow properly. I will fetch you food and drink immediately then."

"Take your time," said the other, smiling. "It is a pleasure to watch the great Mondamay at his work."

"You have heard of me?"

"Who has not heard of your pots—turned to perfection, fired with an amazing glaze?"

Mondamay remained without expression.

"You are kind," he observed.

After a time, Mondamay stopped the wheel and rose to his feet.

"Excuse me," he said.

He moved with a peculiar, shuffling gait. John, his long fingers dipping into a purple pocket, watched the potter's back as he went.

Mondamay entered the cave. Several minutes later, he returned bearing a covered tray.

"I bring you bread and cheese and milk," he said.

"Excuse me if I do not partake of them with you, as I have just eaten."

He bent, graceful for all his bulk, to place the tray before the stranger.

"I will slay a goat for your dinner—" he began.

John's left hand was a blur. His incredibly long fingers dug into the area beneath the other's right shoulder blade. There they penetrated, tearing away a huge flap. His right hand, holding a small crystalline key, was already plunging toward the exposed metallic surface. The key entered a socket there. He turned it.

Mondamay became immobile. A series of sharp clicks occurred somewhere within his stooped form. John withdrew his hand, moved back.

"You are no longer Mondamay the potter," he said. "You have been partially activated, by me. Assume a standing position now."

A soft whirring, accompanied by occasional crackling noises, emerged from the figure before him. Slowly it straightened; then it grew motionless once again.

"Now remove your human disguise."

The figure before him raised its hands slowly to the back of its head. They remained there for a moment, then drew apart and forward, stripping the dark pseudo-flesh from what came to be revealed as a metallic, stepped pyramid set about with numerous lenses. Then the hands moved to what appeared to be the neck, pressed there, pulled downward. Metal. More metal was revealed. And cables, and quartz windows behind which tiny lights flickered, and plates and nozzles and grids...

Within two minutes, all of the false flesh had been stripped away, and the one who had been known as Mondamay stood gleaming, flashing and crackling before the tall man.

"Give me access to Unit One," the man ordered.

Cash register-like, a narrow metal drawer extruded itself from the automaton's chest. John leaned forward, his amethyst rings flashing, and made adjustments upon the controls contained within it.

"Why are you doing this to me?" Mondamay asked him.

"You are now fully activated and must obey me. Is that not correct?"

"Yes, it is. Why have you done this to me?"

"Deaccess Unit One, straighten up and go stand where you were when I arrived."

Mondamay obeyed. The man seated himself and began eating.

"Why have I activated you?" John said after a few moments. "Because," he answered himself, "I am, at the moment, the only man in the world who knows what you are."

"There have been many mistakes concerning me . . ."

"Of that I am certain. I do not know whether there are parallel futures, but I do know that there are many pasts leading up to that time from which I have come. Not all of them are accessible. The sideroads have a way of reverting to wilderness when there are none to travel them. Do you not know that Time is a super-highway with many exits and entrances, main routes and secondary roads, that the maps keep changing, that only a few know how to find the access ramps?"

"I am aware of this, though I am not one who can find his way along them."

"How is it that you know?"

"You are not the first such traveler I have met."

"I know that, here in your branch, a hypothesis which intelligent men find laughable in my own branch happens to be quite true: namely, that the Earth was visited long ago by creatures from another civilization, creatures who left various artifacts behind them. I know you are such an artifact. Is it not so?"

"It is correct."

"I know, further, that you are a fantastically sophis-ticated death machine. You were designed to destroy anything from a single virus to an entire planet. Is that not correct?"

·"It is so."

"You were left behind. And with no one to understand your function, you chose to disguise yourself and lead this simple existence. True?"

"True. How is it that you learned of me and obtained the necessary command key?"

"My employer knows many things. He taught me the ways of the Road. He told me of you. He provided the key."

"And now that you have found me and used it, what is it you wish of me?"

"You said that I am not the first such traveler you have encountered. I know this, for I know the other man's identity. His name is Red Dorakeen, and soon he will be seeking you on this branch. I have need of a very large sum of money, and I will be paid it for killing him. I always prefer working through intermediaries, however—human or mechanical—in matters of violence. You are to be my agent in this matter."

"Red Dorakeen is my friend."

"So I was told. All the less reason for him to suspect you in this. Now—" He rummaged in his pack and withdrew a slim metal case. He opened it and adjusted a pair of knobs. A beeping sound emerged from the unit. "He recently had a windshield replaced," John said, setting the case atop a rock. "When this was done, a small broadcast unit was concealed in his vehicle. Now I have but to wait until he enters this branch, and I can track him with this, striking wherever I choose."

"I do not wish to be your agent in this matter."

John rose from his meal, crossed the area between them, and struck the pot Mondamay had been turning, squashing it out of shape.

"Your wishes are not important," he stated. "You have no choice but to obey me."

"That is true."

"I order you not to attempt to warn him in any way. Do you understand?"

"I do."

"Then do not argue with me about it. You will do as you are told, to the fullest of your ability."

"I will."

John returned to the tray and continued eating.

"I would like to dissuade you from this," Mondamay stated after a time.

"No doubt."

"Do you know why your employer wishes him killed?"

"No. That is his affair. It does not concern me."

"There must be something very special about you, to have warranted your selection for such exotic employment."

John smiled.

"He considered me qualified."

"What do you know of Red Dorakeen?"

"I know what he looks like. I know that he will probably be coming this way."

"You are obviously some sort of professional whom your employer has gone to great lengths to recruit . . ."

"Obviously."

"Have you not wondered why? What is it about your intended victim which requires such consideration?"

"Oh, he wanted me to handle it because the victim may already be aware that he is being hunted."

"How did this come about?"

"Recently, in his personal time-line, there has been one attempt on his life."

"How is it that it failed?"

"Crude, poorly managed, I understand."

"What became of the would-be assassin?"

The man in purple raised his eyes to glare at Mondamay.

"Red killed him. But I assure you there is no comparison to be made between that person and myself."

Mondamay remained silent.

"If you are trying to frighten me, to cause me to feel it could happen to me also, you are wasting your time. There are very few things I fear."

"That is good," said Mondamay.

John remained with Mondamay for the better part of a week, breaking fifty-six delicately wrought pots before discovering that this did not disturb his mechanical servant. Even when he ordered the robot to break them personally, he obtained no equivalent of an emotional response, and so gave up on that avenue as a source of pain to his captive. Then, one afternoon, the bleeping machine emitted a sharp buzzing note. John hurried to adjust it, took a reading, and adjusted it further.

"He is about three hundred kilometers from here," he stated. "As soon as I have bathed and changed my clothing, I will permit you to transport me to him so that this matter may be concluded."

Mondamay did not reply.

One

"Red, that doctor we met back at the repair shop—
I'm a little concerned about what he— Hey! Come on!
You're not going to stop for a hitchhiker when people
are shooting at you!"

"The new speaker is a little strident."

He drew off to the side. Suddenly it was raining. The
small man with the wild hair and the black suitcase
grinned and opened the door.

"How far are you going?" came a high-pitched voice.

"About five Cs."

"Well, that's something, anyway. Nice to get out of
the rain."

He climbed in and slammed the door, balancing the
suitcase on his knees.

"How far are you headed?" Red asked, drawing back
onto the highway.

"Periclean Athens. Jimmy Frazier's the name."

"Red Dorakeen. You've a long haul ahead. How's
your Greek?"

"Been studying it for two years. Always wanted to
make this trip. —I've heard of you."

"Good or bad?"

"Both. And in between. You used to run arms till
they cracked down, didn't you?"

49

Red turned and met the dark eyes which were studying him.

"It's been said."

"Didn't mean to pry."

Red shrugged.

"No secret, I guess."

"You've been in a lot of interesting places, I suppose?"

"Some."

"And some strange ones?"

"A few of those, too."

Frazier combed his hair with his fingers, patted it into place, leaned over to glance at himself in the rearview mirror, sighed.

"I haven't run the Road that much myself. Mainly between Cleveland in the 1950s and Cleveland in the 1980s."

"What do you do?"

"Tend bar, mostly. Also, I buy stuff in the fifties and sell it in the eighties."

"Makes sense."

"Makes money too. —You ever have trouble with hijackers?"

"None to speak of."

"You must have some really fancy armaments on this thing."

"Nothing special."

"I'd think you'd need them."

"Shows how wrong you can be."

"What do you do if you're suddenly up against it?"

Red relit his cigar.

"Maybe die," he replied.

Frazier chuckled.

"No. Really," he said.

Red extended his right arm along the back of the seat.

"Look, if you are a hijacker, you've caught me between loads."

"Me? I'm no hijacker."

"Then stop asking these damn theoretical questions. How the hell should I know what I'd do in some hypothetical situation? I'd respond to circumstances, that's all."

"Sorry. I got carried away. It's a romantic life you lead. Where are you from, originally?"

"I don't know."

"What do you mean?"

"I mean that I can't find my way back. Once it was on the main drag, I think, then it became a byroad probably, then it just disappeared into the misty places which are no longer history. I guess I just waited too long to begin looking. Got occupied. It's not even legend anymore."

"What's it called?"

"Do you smell something burning?"

"Just your cigar."

"My cigar! Where the hell is it?"

"I don't— Here. It seems to have fallen down the seat behind me."

"You get burned?"

"Burned? Oh, I don't think so. Maybe my jacket, a little."

Red accepted the return of his cigar, glanced at the other's back.

"You're lucky then. Sorry."

"You were saying? . . ."

"Red!" Flowers broke in. "There's a police cruiser headed this way."

Frazier started.

"What is that?" he said.

"You should be able to spot it in a minute."

Red regarded the mirror.

"Why don't they go find an accident?" he mused. He glanced at Frazier. "Unless this is some sort of setup."

"What form of magic?—"

". . . Should be coming into view about now."

"Red! Where's that voice coming from?"

"Don't bother me! Damn it!"

"Demons are very untrustworthy!" Frazier said, and he began tracing designs in the air. Fiery shapes flowed from his fingertips and hung before him.

"Red! What's he up to?" Flowers asked. "My optical scanners show—"

Red cut sharply to the right and off onto the shoulder, braking.

"Stop cluttering my cab with spells!" Red ordered. "You're not from any main-branch C Twenty. What are you trying to pull?"

The police cruiser cut past and came to a stop before them. It was a gray evening, and snow decked the trees in the forest to the right.

"I repeat—" Red said, but Frazier had already opened the door and was stepping down.

"I don't know how you managed this—" Frazier began.

Red recognized the officer emerging from the police vehicle but did not know his name.

"—but you have just made a mistake." Frazier regarded the advancing policeman. "So did I, though, come to think of it . . ." he added.

The cab's door slammed shut. The truck went into reverse, its tires grinding gravel. Its wheels cut to the left, its engine revved through a long pause while ghostly shapes streaked by. Then it shot onto the highway to flee through a pale day, a golden arch above it.

"Flowers," Red said, "why did you override?"

"A cost-benefit analysis of that situation put you in the red, Red. There's a better than sixty-percent chance I just saved your life."

"But those were real cops."

"Too bad for them, then."

"He was that dangerous?"

"Think about it."

"I am, and I'm not sure what he was. Wonder where Chadwick got hold of him?"

"He's not one of them. He's not part of the game, Red."

"What makes you think that?"

"He would have been briefed if he were. He didn't even know what I was. Is this Chadwick stupid, to send someone that unprepared?"

"No. You're right. We've got to go back."

"I wouldn't advise it."

"This time I override. Take the next turnoff. Get back on the other side. Then swing around again. I have to know."

"Why?"

"Just do it."

"You're the boss."

The light began to pulse as the truck slowed, then it drew to the right and onto a ramp. Frowning, Red traced designs in the air and then on a pad.

"Yes," he finally said as they headed back.

"Yes, what?"

"Life is getting interesting. Go faster."

"Are you sure you want to find him again?"

"He won't be there."

"You're guessing."

They headed down a ramp, through an underpass, and up again.

"Just a few minutes more. There! Up ahead. The police car is still there. Are you certain we should stop?"

"Do it!"

They pulled off the Road, came to a halt behind the teardrop-shaped vehicle. Red climbed out, walked forward. As he advanced, he could smell burnt upholstery and burnt flesh. The right-hand door of the car was open and slightly twisted. The interior had been thoroughly burned out. The charred body of one man lay sprawled across the front seat, badge blackened, gun in hand. The other officer's remains lay on the ground near the front of the car. The tires had been melted, the rear of the vehicle torn open. Red paced the length of the car several times.

Frazier's suitcase lay sprung on a mound of snowy leaves to his right, its contents strewn on the ground. Red's brow furrowed and he shook his head as he regarded the dildoes, contraceptives, and bondage and discipline devices it had contained. They began to smoke and steam, flow and melt, as he looked at them. He looked about for footprints, but nothing was clear.

Returning to his pickup, he announced, "All right. C Eleven. I'll take over at Twelve, though."

"I could monitor from here. Some sort of bomb, I'd say. Any sign of where he went?"

"No."

"You're lucky."

"Not quite."

"What do you mean?"

"Well, we let it get away."

"I'd call that lucky."

Red yanked his cap down over his eyes and folded his arms. His breathing deepened.

Two

Timyin Tin worked in the monastery garden, apologizing to the weeds as he removed them. A small man, whose shaven head made his age even more difficult to determine, he hoed with great enthusiasm, his movements sharp and supple. His gown hung loosely about him, occasionally disturbed by the cool wind from the snow-capped mountains. He seldom looked at the mountains. He knew them too well. He was instantly alert to the approach of a fellow monk, however, though he gave no sign of this awareness until the other came to a halt at the head of the row he was working.

"You are wanted within," said the other.

Timyin Tin nodded.

"Good-bye, my friends," he said to the plants, and he went to clean his tools and place them in the shed.

"The garden grows well," the other said.

"Yes."

"I believe this summons involves the visitors."

"Oh? I heard the gong earlier, announcing the arrival of travelers, but I did not see who had come."

"Their names are Sundoc and Toba. Do you know them?"

"No."

The two men passed toward the main building, pausing briefly before a statue of the Buddha. They entered and moved along a hall to a cell near its end. The second man entered there with proper observances and addressed the small, shriveled man who was the head of the monastery.

"He is here, worthy one."

"Then bid him enter."

He returned to the doorway, barely glancing at the two strangers who sat on mats across from the master, drinking tea.

"You may come in," he said, withdrawing himself as Timyin Tin entered the cell.

"You sent for me, honored sir," he said.

The master regarded him for several moments before speaking.

"These gentlemen wish you to accompany them on a journey," he finally said.

"Myself, esteemed one? There are many who know the area far better."

"Of this I am aware, but it seems they want more than a guide. I will leave it to them to make matters clear to you."

With this, the master rose to his feet, carrying with him a saddlebag that clinked and rattled, and departed the cell.

Both strangers stood as Timyin Tin regarded them.

"My name is Toba," said the dark-skinned one with the beard. He was heavily built and stood perhaps a head taller than Timyin Tin. "My companion is called Sundoc." He indicated the very tall, copper-haired man, whose skin was pale, whose eyes were blue. "His fourteenth-century Chinese of this district is not as good as my own, so I will speak for both of us. Who are you, Timyin Tin?"

"I do not understand," the monk replied. "I am he whom you see before you."

Toba laughed. A moment later, Sundoc laughed also.

"Forgive us," Toba said then. "But what were you before you came to this place? Where did you live? What did you do?"

The monk spread his hands.

"I do not remember."

"You work in the gardens here. Do you like that?"

"Yes. Very much."

Toba shook his head.

"How are the mighty fallen," he said. "Do you think—"

The larger man had taken a step nearer the monk. His fist suddenly shot forward.

Timyin Tin appeared to shift only slightly, but Sundoc's fist passed him without making contact. The fingers of the monk's left hand seemed but to graze the passing elbow to guide it. His body turned somewhat. His other hand disappeared behind the larger man.

Sundoc was swept across the room to crash into the wall, head-downward. He fell to the floor and lay still.

"Ex—" Toba began. Then he, too, lay on the floor, senseless.

When the light returned to his eyes, Toba looked about the cell. The monk stood near the door, regarding him.

"Why did he attack me?" Timyin Tin asked.

"It was but a test," Toba gasped. "It is now ended and you have passed it. Do they practice such unarmed combat here?"

"Some," the monk said. "But I knew much from— before."

"Tell me about before. Where was it? When?"

Timyin Tin shook his head.

"I do not know."

"Another life, perhaps?"

"Perhaps."

"You believe in such things here—having lived other lives, do you not?"

"Yes."

Toba got to his feet. Across the chamber, Sundoc sighed and stirred.

"We wish you no harm," Toba said. "Quite the contrary. You must accompany us on a journey. It is very important. The head of your order has agreed to this."

"Where are we to go?"

"The place names would be meaningless to you at this time."

"What is it that you want me to do in the place where we are to go?"

"You would not understand that either, in your present condition. A different you—an earlier incarnation—would have. Have you never wondered about the man you once might have been?"

"I have wondered."

"We will restore these memories to you."

"How were they taken away?"

"By sophisticated chemical and neurological techniques you would not understand. You see, even to mention them, I have had to use words which are not in your present vocabulary."

"You know what I was—before?"

"Yes."

"Tell me what I was like."

"It is better for you to discover it for yourself. We will assist you."

"How will you do this?"

"We will give you a series of injections of— You would not know what RNA is, but we will treat you with your own RNA, from samples taken before you were changed."

"This substance will return knowledge of my earlier life to me?"

"We think so. Sundoc is a highly skilled physician. He will administer it."

"I do not know . . ."

"What do you mean?"

"I am not certain that I wish to become acquainted with the man I once was. What if I do not like him?"

Sundoc, who had risen to his feet and stood rubbing his head, smiled.

Toba said, "I can tell you this: You did not undergo the first change willingly."

"Why would someone force me to become another man?"

"There is only one way for you to learn this. What do you say?"

Timyin Tin crossed the cell to the urn and poured himself a cup of tea. He seated himself upon a mat and stared into the cup. He took a sip. After a time, Sundoc and Toba also settled to the floor.

"Yes, it is frightening," Toba said finally, groping for words and shaping them slowly. "It is the— uncertainty. You seem to have adjusted well to life here. Now we come along and offer to change it all, without really telling you what the alternative will be. This is not perversity on our part. In your present state of mind, you simply would not understand what we have to say. We are asking you to accept a strange gift—your own past—because we wish to talk with the man you used to be. It may be that, when you have remembered, you will not choose to deal with us. Then, of course, you would be free to go your own way, to return here if you wish. But the gift we will have given you is not a thing we can recall."

"Self-knowledge is a thing I desire," Timyin Tin stated, "and the recollection of past lives is an important step along that road. For this reason, I should say yes immediately. But I have meditated upon just this in the past. Supposing I were to achieve recall of a previous existence—not just a few memories, but all of it? Supposing I not only did not like that individual, but discovered that he was stronger than I—and instead of assimilating him into my existence, he were to assimilate me? What then? Would it not be a turning backward of the Great Wheel? By accepting knowledge from a source I do not understand, may I not be laying myself open to such possession by an earlier self?"

Neither man answered him, and he took another sip of tea.

"But why should I ask you?" he said then. "No man can answer such a question for another."

"Yet," said Toba, "it is a fair question. Of course, I cannot answer it for you. I can only suggest that, in terms of your beliefs, one of your future selves may one day be wondering that same thing about you. What would your feelings be about that?"

Abruptly, Timyin Tin laughed.

"Very good," he said. "The self always wants to be at the center of things, does it not?"

"You've got me."

Timyin Tin finished his tea, and when he looked up, there was a new expression on his face. It was difficult to understand how that slight squint with the small rising of the cheeks above a half-smile could convey the sense of recklessness, boldness and defiance that it did.

"I am ready for this enlightenment," he announced. "Let it begin."

"It will probably take many days," Toba said cautiously. "There must be a number of treatments."

"Then there must be a first one," Timyin Tin said. "What am I to do?"

Sundoc glanced at Toba. Toba nodded.

"All right, we will begin the treatments now," Sundoc stated. He rose and moved to the corner of the cell where his gear was stacked. "How soon can you be ready to travel?" he asked.

"My possessions are few," the monk replied. "As soon as this business is concluded, I will fetch my things and we can depart."

"Good," said the tall man, opening a small case containing a syringe and a number of ampules. "Good."

*   *   *

That night they camped in the mountains high above the monastery. They had sought a rocky declivity which broke the howling winds. Fine grains of snow swirled about their small campfire—like souls rushing to be melted, vaporized, returned to the heavens—recast, thought Timyin Tin—and he regarded them for a long while after the others had retired.

In the morning, he said to Toba, "I had a strange dream."

"What was it?"

"I dreamed there were some men in a vehicle of a sort with which I am not familiar. I was in a building, watching as it came to a halt. When the men emerged from it, I pointed a weapon at them—a tube with a handle and a small lever. I directed it toward them and drew back on the lever. They were destroyed. Could this dream be a part of my other life?"

"I do not know for certain," Toba said, gathering and packing his gear. "It could be. At this time, it is better not to regard any such things too critically. It is best simply to let them fall into place by themselves."

Timyin Tin received an injection before they decamped and another that evening, following many leagues' travel along mountain trails.

"I feel that something is happening," he said. "There were peculiar—intrusions—into my thoughts today."

"What sort of intrusions?"

"Images, words . . ."

Sundoc drew nearer.

"What images?" he asked.

Timyin Tin shook his head.

"Too brief, too fleeting. I can no longer recall them."

"And the words? . . ."

"They were foreign, though they seemed familiar. I no longer recall any of them, either."

"You may take it as a good sign," Sundoc said. "The treatments are beginning to work. You may have more strange dreams tonight. Do not let them trouble you. It is best simply to observe and to learn."

That night Timyin Tin did not sit up meditating.

On the second morning, there was something different in his manner. When questioned by Toba concerning dreams, he simply replied, "Fragments."

"Fragments? What were they like?"

"I cannot remember. Nothing important. Let's have the morning's shot, huh?"

"Do you realize that the last thing you said was not spoken in Chinese?"

Timyin Tin's eyes widened. He looked away. He looked down at his feet. He looked back at Toba.

"No," he said. "It just came out that way."

His eyes filled with tears.

"What is happening to me? Who will win?"

"You will be the ultimate winner, by regaining what you had lost."

"But perhaps—" Then his expression changed. His eyes narrowed, the lines of his cheeks softened, a faint smile curved the corner of his lips. "Of course," he said, "and I thank you for it.

"How far must we journey?" he asked then.

"It is difficult to explain," Toba said, "but we should be out of these mountains in three days. Then perhaps a week's travel will take us to a major trail we must follow. It will be much easier after that, but the exact destination will depend on word we receive at a rest stop along the way. Let us give you your treatment now and begin."

"Very well."

That evening and the following day, Timyin Tin did not speak of whatever recollections might have come to him. When asked, he was vague. Sundoc and Toba did not press the matter. The treatments continued. The next afternoon, however, as they were making their way down through a pass toward the foothills, Timyin Tin pulled upon their sleeves to gain their attention.

"We are being followed," he whispered. "Continue on as if all is well. I will join you later."

"Wait!" said Toba. "I do not want you to take any risks. You see, we have weapons of a sort you do not understand. We—"

He stopped, for the smaller man was smiling.

"Really?" Timyin Tin said. "Are you quite certain about that? No, I fear that your firearms would not help you against a storm of arrows from above. As I said, I will join you shortly."

He turned and vanished among the rocks to their right.

"What shall we do?" Toba asked.

"What he told us: continue on," Sundoc replied. "The man is no fool."

"But he is not in a normal state of mind."

"It is obvious that he remembers more than he has said. We must trust him now. Actually, we haven't much of a choice."

They continued on.

Almost an hour passed. The wind fled about them and the echoes of their mounts' hoofs sounded against the rocky walls. Twice, Sundoc had dissuaded Toba from returning to search for their charge. Now his face, too, was tight, and his eyes shifted often toward the heights. Both men were more than normally hunched as they rode.

"If we've lost him," Toba said, "we are in deep trouble."

The larger man's voice did not carry conviction as he replied, "We haven't lost him."

They rode a little farther and a dark object fell to the trail some distance before them. It bounced, then rolled, giving, for a moment, the appearance of a rock. Then they noticed the hair. Shortly thereafter, the torso struck the ground. Two entire bodies followed moments later.

They drew rein just as a shout echoed about them.

Seeking its source, they saw Timyin Tin atop a crag high above them to the right. He waved a saber, placed it upon the ground, then commenced climbing down the rocky wall.

"I told you we hadn't lost him," Sundoc said.

When the smaller man had completed his descent and approached them, Toba shifted and frowned.

"You took unnecessary risks," he said. "You do not know what weapons we have with us. We could have helped you. Three against one are not good odds."

Timyin Tin smiled faintly.

"There were seven," he replied. "Only three were so positioned that they were borne over the edge. But I took no unnecessary chances, and your weapons would only have gotten in the way."

Sundoc whistled softly. Toba shook his head.

"We were worried. Whatever your prowess, your mind is not yet normal."

"In this it is," the other replied. "Shall we continue our journey?"

They rode for a long while without speaking, then Sundoc asked, "How do you feel now?"

Timyin Tin nodded.

"All right."

"Yet you have been frowning, as if something troubles you. Has this to do with this afternoon's—conflict?"

"Yes, I am somewhat troubled by what occurred."

"It is understandable. That part of you which is a monk—"

The smaller man shook his head violently.

"No! That is not it! We may kill in self-defense, and this was surely that. My concern runs deeper than the act and its justifications, karmic or otherwise."

"What, then?"

"I did not know that it lay within me to derive pleasure from it. I see now that I should have taken warning from the dreams."

"This pleasure was great?"

"Yes."

"Might it not have been pride for the success of your expedition?"

"It grew very much within that place, yet its roots ran deeper still—to some other place where there are no reasons, only feelings. I have been examining it, as I have learned to question my motives, and I can go no further than the simple fact of its existence. It has given me wonder, however . . ."

"Of what sort?"

"When whatever was done to me was done, making me forget who I had been and what I had wrought, there must have been a good reason. Could it have been that I was a threat, that I represented a danger as I was?"

"I will be honest with you, rather than keep you wondering and worrying," Sundoc said. "Yes, this was the case. But you must realize, too, that you were not destroyed when you could have been. There was also that about you which was considered worth saving."

"But what was it?" Timyin Tin said. "Was it a hidden measure of moral worth some benign prince wished to see nurtured, to balance other things I might have been? Or was it rather that he did not wish to destroy what had once proved a useful tool?"

"Perhaps something of both," Sundoc said, "plus being in your debt."

"The memories of princes are generally short. But be that as it may, I see only one special item in my repertoire for which one such might desire my recall. Whoever sent you here wants me to kill someone, does he not?"

"I think these are matters best to be discussed at a later date, when your treatment has been completed."

Sundoc moved to shake his mount's reins, but Timyin Tin's hand had somehow grasped them before that action could be completed.

"Now," the smaller man said. "I want to know now.

I possess a sufficient degree of self-awareness to understand a simple yes or no answer to my question."

Sundoc looked into his dark eyes, looked away.

"And if the answer is yes?"

"Try it and we'll see."

"Look, I am not the proper person to be making
you any proposals. Why don't you wait until we get
to where we are going? You will be more in control of
yourself and there will be someone there who—"

"Yes or no?" he said as Toba drew up beside them.

Sundoc looked at the other man, who nodded.

"All right. Yes, someone wants a man dead and
thinks that you are the best man for the job. That is
why we came for you."

The smaller man released the reins.

"That is sufficient for now," he said. "I am not interested in the details yet."

"Well, what is your reaction to the information?"
Toba asked.

"It is nice to be wanted," Timyin Tin replied. "Let
us be on our way."

"You heard the words with equanimity. How interested do you feel you would be in such an undertak-
ing?"

"Very," he said, "since it must be intricate to warrant
my resurrection. I wonder more, though, about another thing."

"What is that?"

"I am strong, and I grow stronger as the treatments
progress. But the monk is still with me. I wonder
whether this will always be so?"

"Yes, for he is but another of your own faces."

"Good. I would hate to lose contact entirely with
this part of my life. It was—peaceful. Only . . . I may
now be equipped with a strange sort of conscience."

"Let us hope that it does not get in the way."

"It depends entirely on what you are asking of me."

"You said that you were not interested in the details."

"That was someone else talking."

"Very well. There is a Road and it goes on forever, and a man with a certain affinity for it, a man who knows the proper entrances and exits, twists and turnings, may follow it to almost any time or place. Of the many who go that route, there is one against whom the black decade has been declared—"

"Black decade?"

"His enemy is permitted ten attempts on his life, without warning. These may take any form. Agents may be employed."

"And your master wishes me to be such an agent?"

"Yes."

"Why the black decade in the first place? What has this man done?"

"I really do not know. It is likely, however, that you will never even see him. One of the others will probably get him first—if that will give your conscience some peace."

"Do you mean to say that you are going to all this trouble to set me up as a backup man?"

"That's right. This man is deemed worth the effort."

"If the others' skills approach my own, he has no chance of getting past the first. But what happens if he does live through all the assaults?"

"I am not sure anyone ever has."

"But this one is special?"

"So I am told. Very special."

"I see. Let us make camp soon, for I must meditate."

"Of course. Such a decision is not made lightly."

"I have already made the decision. I now wish to know whether I have been insulted or honored."

They rode past the bodies. The sun broke from behind a cloud. The wind came up into their faces.

One

Red drove slowly along the dirt road. The next rest stop, with its stone and log buildings, would be the last on the route he had taken in this C Eleven Africa. Turning into the parking area, he drew up beside a streamlined pearl-gray ground-effect vehicle.

"That one's from pretty far up the line," he observed. "Wonder whose it is?"

He removed Flowers from her compartment, took a rifle down from the rack behind him and opened the door. Stepping out, he groped beneath the seat and located a knife in a leather sheath. He fastened it to his belt and locked the cab. Raising a backpack from the bed of the truck, he opened and inspected it.

"Everything I need but water," he announced, "and maybe a paperback. I want to go inside anyhow, to tell them I'll be parked here for a while."

"It's kind of late in the day, and you've done a lot of driving. Maybe you ought to lay over and start in the morning."

He looked at the sky.

"I could still get in a few good hours of legwork."

" . . . And then go to all the trouble of making camp, to spend an extra night on the trail. Is it going to make that much difference?"

"I don't know."

" . . . You could probably use a good meal too."

"On that, you're right," he said, shouldering the rifle and hefting the pack, to which he had added Flowers. "We'll go see what's on the menu and find out what sort of accommodations they have. If neither one is very good I might as well be on the trail, though."

He moved off in the direction of the main building. The proprietor, an elderly man with a French accent, and his wife—young, heavy, native—sat in wicker chairs in the reception area, beneath a large fan. He smiled, put down a book and a drink, and rose as Red entered.

"Hello. May I serve you?"

"Hi. I'm Red. Dorakeen. I was wondering what may be available for dinner."

"Peter Laval. And this is Betty. A stew—native meats, carefully seasoned. Beer made here, or wine brought in, to go with it. You may inspect the kitchen, sniff the pot, if you choose."

"Not necessary. I'm getting a whiff here. Smells good. What are the rooms like?"

"Come take a look. Right around the corner."

Red followed him down a short hall and into a small, clean room.

"Not bad. I'll take it," he said, lowering his pack to the floor after removing and pocketing Flowers and placing the rifle on the bed. He tossed his jacket down beside it.

" . . . And I wouldn't mind some of that beer now."

"This way. I'll get you a key too, if you want one."

Red followed him back into the hall, closing the door behind him.

"Might as well. Many other guests?"

"No, just yourself today. Things are slow—as usual."

"That fancy car out there yours?"

"No, mine is in back, and much less pretentious."

"Whose is it, then?" Red asked as they approached

a desk where he signed a guest book and received a key.

"Ah! You are reading Baudelaire! One of my favorites. There was a man who saw through pretensions—everything! *'Combla-t-il sur ta chair inerte et complaisante l'immensité de son désir?'* "

" *' . . . Réponds, cadavre impur!'* " Red said, nodding, following the other into a small taproom, where a stein was drawn for him. "Whose car is it?"

Laval chuckled, leading him out onto the veranda and gesturing toward the mountains.

"A most unusual fellow," he said. "Hiked off in that direction last week. Big, skinny, with eyes like Rasputin . . . Hands such as Modigliani might have painted somewhere or other. And every stitch on him, down to his bootlaces, was green. Even had on a big emerald ring. Didn't say where he was going or why. Said his name was John, that's all."

Flowers emitted a small squeak. Red thumbed the piezoelectric acknowledgment point.

". . . And to tell the truth, I was glad to see him go. He didn't do anything threatening or even uncivil. But he made me uncomfortable just being here."

Red sipped his beer.

"I've left my drink inside. Would you care to join us in the lobby? It's a little cooler there."

Red shook his head.

"I'm enjoying the view from here. Thanks anyway."

Laval shrugged and withdrew. Red raised Flowers.

"Yeah, I caught it," he muttered. "I suppose it could be the same guy. Indicating—"

"It's not that," said the tiny voice, "though it could be. But it *is* what caused me to set up surveillance. I decided to run periodic reconnaissance surveys through the truck's sensors via microwave. I've picked something up."

"What?"

"Electrical activity associated with something approaching from the southwest. It's easy to spot against this quiet background. It's coming up pretty fast."

"How large an object is it?"

"I can't tell yet."

Red took another drink.

"Conclusions? Recommendations?"

"Go get your rifle and keep it with you. Maybe a grenade. I don't know what you've got on you. I've already broadcast a message to that doctor we met."

"Then you *do* think it's his man?"

"You have to admit it sounds that way. Let us not take chances."

"I'm not arguing."

Red set his stein on a ledge, turned toward his truck.

"Uh-oh, Flowers," he announced. "Something airborne from that direction, and it ain't no bird."

"I'm tracking. That's it. You might still be able to get the rifle, if you run."

"Oh, the hell with it," Red said, unwrapping a fresh cigar and lighting it. "It would just get in the way. You might get a chance to try that brand-new routine, though."

He retrieved his beer and seated himself on the edge of the veranda.

"I've had an acknowledgment from the physician. He is near, and he's on his way."

"Great."

He opened Flowers and read a few lines.

"I must say, you're taking it very philosophically."

"Well, isn't this the way to go—with a drink, a cigar and a good book?"

"The preparations do not seem entirely adequate."

"Maybe this is my place . . . And I've already caught a glimpse of the opposition."

"And? . . ."

"Here they come now."

The robot soared above the parking lot, slowing. The man, clad all in yellow now, rode upon its back. It continued to slow, gradually assumed a vertical attitude, then descended gently to the ground, landing perhaps fifteen meters from the veranda.

Red sipped his beer and set it down. He rose to his feet, smiling, and took a step forward.

"Hi, Mondy," he said. "Who's your friend?"

"Red . . ." Mondamay began.

"Silence!" said John, stepping down and stretching. His topaz rings flashed in the sunlight. "Remain in position! Battle systems active!"

He stepped forward and bowed from the waist.

"John will do. And you, I take it, are Red Dorakeen?"

"That is correct. Anything I can do for you?"

"As a matter of fact, yes. You can die. Mondamay—"

"A moment. May I inquire as to your purpose in this?"

John paused in mid-gesture, nodded sharply.

"Very well. I wish to assure you that there is absolutely nothing personal involved. I am simply carrying out a commission in order to earn a large sum of money, which I require to further various personal ambitions. A man named Chadwick hired me to do this. Ah! You nod. But then you had already guessed, hadn't you? Former friends can make the worst enemies. Pity. But there you are. I won't point any morals. It's a little late for them to be of much use to you."

"So you accepted the commission, determined my destination and located a complicated piece of equipment to do the work for you? . . ."

"That pretty much summarizes things. Chadwick put my feet on the right track—"

"I wonder whether your reliance on an agent is a mark of fear?"

"Fear? No more than Chadwick's hiring me is an indication of fear on his part. He is a very busy man.

He sought to employ efficiency, as do I . Do you think I fear to fight you, or any man?"

Red smiled.

"No," John said, noting the smile. "You shan't goad me into giving you an unearned chance at life. Your opinion of me means nothing when I know better."

Red puffed on his cigar.

"Interesting," he said. "Then I suppose it is merely of academic interest to you that the man who told me about you is even now approaching?"

"Man? What man?"

Red glanced at the roadway.

"A big golden-eyed guy with one hell of a suntan," he said. "I met him at a rest stop back on the Road. Driving a hot little 1920s roadster. Had on a torn shirt. Said he was going to do a lobotomy on you with an icepick."

"I don't believe you!"

Red shrugged.

"Why don't you ask him yourself? I believe that's the roadster approaching now."

John turned to regard a rushing vehicle, dust boiling behind it. Red took several steps forward.

"Halt! Right there!" John spun and raised one hand, his eyes flashing. "If this is a trick, it won't work. And if it is not, I welcome the opportunity to kill that bird with this same stone. Mondamay! Burn Red Dorakeen down to a cinder!"

Mondamay raised his right arm, extruding a tube which he pointed at Red. Lights flashed in the vicinity of his shoulder. There came a crackling sound. A tiny wisp of smoke curled upward from out of the tube.

"Shorted again," he declared.

"What do you mean 'again'?" John said.

"It's been that way for thousands of years."

"Then disintegrate him! Blow him up! Bomb him! I don't care how you do it!"

A whirring sound began deep within Mondamay.

His lights flashed rapidly. Clicking noises emerged from various units. A tiny whine began somewhere.

"Uh—John," Red said, "did you never stop to wonder why that alien race left a piece of complicated equipment like Mondamay behind?"

"I'd rather assumed it was for purposes of knocking us back to barbarism if our civilization took some turn of which they disapproved."

"Naw, nothing that sophisticated," Red said. "Massive systems failures. He couldn't be repaired, so they abandoned him. Felt a little sorry for him since he was sentient, so they left him with his hobbies and his disguises. After all, he was harmless—"

"Mondamay! Is that true?"

Smoke was emerging from all of Mondamay's joints, and the whine had risen to a wail. The lights still flashed, the clanking was constant now.

"Afraid so, John," he replied. "I guess I just burned one world too many in my younger days—"

"Why didn't you tell me this?"

"You never asked me."

Red moved forward again.

"And so," he said, "you will have to earn your fee the hard way."

John turned back toward him, a smile on his lips.

"So be it. You get your wish and I get my hands dirty," he said, moving to meet him. "I will even save you the trouble of anticipating me by telling you how I will proceed. I am going to raise you above the ground by the neck, hold you at arm's length and strangle you with one hand while you dangle there. I would not imagine you think me cap—"

His eyes widened and he halted. He raised both hands slowly to his face.

"What—?"

"You never asked me whether *I* cared to get *my* hands dirty," Red said, turning Flowers slowly to follow John's collapse. "I don't."

John fell and lay still. A trickle of blood emerged from his left ear.

"See? I'd always wanted that speaker with the ultra-sound range," Flowers observed, "and if you'd gotten me the better model, you wouldn't even have had to edge up this close."

Red went to Mondamay, turned and withdrew the crystal key, and was handing it to him as the roadster came into the parking lot.

"You'd better keep this thing in a safe place or destroy it," he said.

"I was not even aware that this one existed," Mondamay replied. "Perhaps it was specially manufactured, or maybe it comes from some other branch of the Road. I barely recognized you. You look younger. What—"

John moaned and began to rise. Red leaned over and struck him on the jaw. He fell again.

"Well, all's well now," Red said. "I was just coming to visit you."

The car had braked to a halt. Its door slammed.

"How pleasant—"

"Hold Flowers a moment, would you? I want to speak with this gentleman."

Red turned toward the giant figure with the black bag who was now striding toward him.

"Hello again. Sorry to trouble you if we were mistaken," he said, glancing down, "but is this the guy you were looking for?"

The big man nodded and opened his bag.

"He is. Are you all right?"

"Can't complain. He's just had an ultrasound jolt and a left to the jaw, though."

The golden-eyed man examined John's ears and eyes, listened to his heartbeat. He filled a syringe from an ampule, knelt and gave him a large injection in the right biceps. He drew a pair of handcuffs from his hip pocket and fastened John's hands behind his back. He then proceeded to search the yellow-clad form, removing various small devices from cuffs, collars, sleeves and boots.

"That about does it," he said, closing his bag and rising. "As I told you before, he is a very dangerous man. What did you do to warrant his attentions?"

"He was hired to get me."

"Then someone must want you very badly, to pay the sort of fee he'd charge."

"I know. I'm going to have to do something about it pretty soon."

The other regarded him for a moment.

"If you would like my help in resolving this matter, I will be glad to give you a hand."

Red drew his teeth across his lower lip and slowly shook his head.

"Thanks, Doc. I appreciate it. But no thanks. This is a very special sort of thing."

The big man smiled faintly and nodded.

"You know your situation best."

He stooped and raised the supine figure effortlessly with one arm. His shirt tore across his back as he did so. Slinging John over his shoulder, he turned and extended his hand.

"Thanks for my patient then, and best of luck with your—problem."

"Thanks. Good-bye, Doc."

"Good-bye."

He watched the other walk back to his car, deposit his burden, get in and drive off.

"Good to see John get his," said Mondamay, extending a metal hand, the firing tube now retracted, and placing it on Red's shoulder. "By the way, he was able to monitor your progress by means of a broadcasting device secreted somewhere on your vehicle. It was placed there at a repair shop you recently visited. He'd mentioned it to me. Perhaps we had best locate it and remove it before we do anything else."

"Good idea. Let's have a look." They moved off toward the truck. "How come you didn't detect it, Flowers?"

"Must be an odd wavelength. I don't know. I'll start a scan."

"You did not introduce me," Mondamay said.

"Huh? Oh, he was so busy with John that I didn't want to interrupt him."

"Not the doctor. Flowers of Evil, here. I did not realize I was holding a sophisticated intelligence when you handed me a book."

"Sorry. Extenuating circumstances. Mondamay, I want you to meet Flowers of Evil. Flowers, this is Mondamay the killing machine."

"I am pleased," Mondamay said.

"Likewise. I find your plight extremely distressing—carrying around all those dead circuits, being deprived of function."

"Oh, it's not all that bad. I enjoy what I'm doing just as much as what I used to do."

"What is that?"

"I'm a potter, among other things. Any sort of precision work in the arts appeals to me."

"How fascinating. I think I'm almost ready for some degree of manual ability myself. At least I'd like to try. I'd love to see your pots sometime—"

"Flowers," Red asked, "have you spotted the broadcast unit yet?"

"Yes. It's affixed to the underside of the body a little forward of the left rear tire."

"Thanks."

Red moved to the rear of the truck and crouched. "You're right," he said after a moment. "Here it is."

Detaching the device, he crossed to the front of the ground-effect car and fastened it to a spot within the front bumper. He returned then to where Mondamay stood leafing through Flowers.

"Just to let them know we caught it," he said.

". . . And this *Paysage* is certainly a lovely one," Mondamay was saying.

"Thank you."

"It's nearly dinnertime," Red said. "Come keep me company and tell me how things have been. I've a lot I want to ask you."

"Delighted," Mondamay replied. "By the way, I'm sorry about this whole business."

"Not your fault. But I'd be grateful for some advice on it."

"Certainly. And I'm anxious to hear your story."

"Let's go then."

"Don't send a charge up there! It's called a tickle circuit . . . Stop it!"

Red halted.

"Huh?"

"Sorry. Didn't realize I was vocalizing. Flowers was curious about one of my subunits."

"Oh."

They crossed the veranda and entered the building.

Two

It was over. Randy had driven Julie to the bus station that morning, helped her with her bags, said good-bye. By now she was well on her way to her parents' home in Virginia. There was nothing of hers in sight in the apartment's small living room or kitchen, between which he wandered, preparing fresh glasses of iced tea and drinking them. He had taken the last of his final exams the previous day and gone with Julie to a good restaurant for a late dinner. He had even gotten a bottle of fine wine to go with it. Neither of them had said it was over, but the feeling was there. Now she was on her way back to Virginia, and he had to line something up for the summer. She had wanted him to go home with her; she'd said that her father could find him a summer job. But Randy had smelled a trap in this. He did not want any strings on him yet. The arrangement they had had was fine, with an agreement as to its temporary nature from the beginning. But she had tried to change the rules with her offer, and he was not ready for anything like that. In the back of his mind, thoughts of the search still lurked, though postponement had weakened that childhood resolution. And there was school. And all the things he wanted to do before he even thought about settling down. No. She

had offered. He had refused. Something had changed.
A different feeling was there. It was over.

He moved to the window and looked three blocks
through the evening in the direction of the campus. He
wore a T-shirt, Bermuda shorts and thong sandals.
People on the street below were similarly clad. It had
been a bright-skied, humid day with more such days
forecast to follow. His arms and legs were coppery beneath scribblings of reddish hair. He drew the back of
his hand across his broad forehead and it came away
wet. He held the glass against his cheek and regarded
the storefronts, parked cars, passing cars, bicycles. Insects still hummed within the trees. An orange cat
licked at a melting ice cream cone on the sidewalk
below.

Over . . . He could work in construction again if he
wanted to return to Cleveland. But that was bad too.
He might have to live at home—Mr. Schelling had even
gone out of his way to say how much they wanted
him to—and that was no damn good. Even if he managed to get a place of his own, they would be after him.
He had only met the man twice and could not bring
himself to call him anything but "Mr. Schelling," even
though he had been married to Randy's mother for almost six months now. It was not that he disliked him.
It was just that he did not know him and did not care
to. No, not back there. That was over too.

He sipped his tea and turned toward the bedroom.
Too hot to think. They had been out late the night
before and up early this morning. Sprawl on the bed
and hope for a breeze, and maybe an idea would come
for a summer job for a classics major. Or would it be
linguistics in the fall? Or Romance languages? It
would be neat to travel abroad as a secretary, an in-
terpreter . . .

As he passed the bookcase, his hand moved without
premeditation and drew out the copy of *Leaves of
Grass*.

Then it *had* been in the back of his mind—the search, the promise . . .

He carried the book with him into the bedroom. He needed something to fill his mind in there. Maybe that was all there was to it.

He propped himself up with pillows, turned the pages and read. It was strange, though, the fascination the book held for him. He had consciously had to avoid it this past quarter, for it had attracted him each time he'd passed the bookcase. It was the only thing he owned that had belonged to his father.

It was dark when he finished reading, and the bedside lamp burned beside him. The moist rings from his glass had not evaporated, but lay like Venn diagrams upon the nightstand. He thought about his father, whom he had never seen. Paul Carthage had lived with his mother briefly and departed before Nora even knew she was pregnant. Where was he now? He could be dead. He could be anywhere. Randy turned to the back of the book, where he kept the only photo he had of him. A monochrome, it showed a wide-shouldered, large-handed man with a mass of curly hair; he had a heavy brow over rough but regular features, and he was smiling despite the fact that he looked uncomfortable in the light suit and tie. Transportation . . . He had told Nora he was in transportation. That could mean anything from a cab dispatcher to an airline pilot. Randy sought himself in that face, looked away with recognition. He had to find him. He wanted to see him and talk with him and learn what he was, where he had come from, what he did, whether he had sired others and what they were like. Paul Carthage . . . He wondered whether that was even his real name. But there were no clues Randy had ever been able to uncover. When he had departed that night in his blue Dodge pickup truck, the only things he had left behind were his marked-up copy of *Leaves of Grass* and an embryonic Randy.

He replaced the photo and closed the book, hefting it. It was heavier than it looked. In one place where the green binding had worn, it appeared that the cover board was of a light metal. He opened it and paged through again. There was no apparent pattern to the underlinings at first glance. But he began with the first that he found and moved through the book, reading them aloud, a thing he had not done before. Odd that he had never thought to trace, in these sections, some aspect of his father's sensibilities. What was it that had moved him to mark the passages that he had? Of course, there was always the possibility that it was a used book, purchased in this condition. Still . . . Something in the sections appealed to Randy beyond the mere tingle of familiarity. There was a wildness, a freedom, a restlessness that seemed to speak to him personally, to reach after some similar place in his own spirit . . . "Is it only because I am twenty years old?" he wondered. "Would I feel this way if I came across this book ten years from now?" He shrugged and continued reading.

A tiny breeze stirred the curtain. He paused and drew in a deep breath. A small wave of coolness passed him. What was he doing? Reading to forget Julie, or to reopen the case on his father? Both, actually, he decided . . . Both. But now that he had begun thinking of the search, he wanted to go on with it.

The breeze was the first bit of coolness in two days. He lay there with his finger marking his place, trying to breathe it all in before it was used up. It was a relief and . . .

He raised his left hand and regarded his fingertips. He rubbed them against his palm. He touched the book's cover once again.

Warm.

He touched the bedding at his side. Perhaps it was just his body heat that had done it . . .

He reached out and pressed his fingers against the glass on the nightstand. Cooler there. Yes . . .

After about half a minute, he touched the book's cover.

It did seem warmer than it should be. He held it close to his face. The faintest of vibrations seemed to be coming from the volume. He pressed his ear against the back cover. It seemed to be present there, too. It was such a gentle, subaural thing, however, that it could almost be his tired nerves playing games with background sensations.

He reopened the book to the point where he had stopped and sought the next marked passage. It was from "Song of the Open Road":

You road I enter upon and look around, I believe
you are not all that is here,
I believe that much unseen is also here.

As he read this, the book vibrated in his hand and emitted a definite, audible, humming sound. It was as though the cover were some sort of resonator.

"What the hell!"

He dropped it. The book lay beside him and a voice said, "Query. Query." It seemed to be coming from the book itself.

He drew over to the far side of the bed and swung his legs to the floor. Then he looked back. The volume had not moved.

Finally, "Did you speak?" he said.

"Yes," came the voice—soft, feminine.

"What are you?"

"I am a microdot computer array. Specifications—"

"You are the book? The book I was just reading?"

"I am arrayed in the form of a book. That is correct."

"Did you belong to my father?"

"Insufficient information. Who are you?"

"Randy Blake. I believe my father was Paul Carthage."

"Tell me about yourself, and how I came into your possession."

"I was twenty this past March. You were left behind by my father in Cleveland, Ohio, before I was born."

"Where are we now?"

"Kent, Ohio."

"Randy Blake—or Carthage, as the case may be—I cannot tell whether or not I belonged to your father."

"Who did you belong to?"

"He used a number of different names."

"Was Paul Carthage one of them?"

"Not that I know of. But this, of course, proves nothing."

"True. Well, what turned you on, anyway?"

"A mnemonic key. I have been set to respond when certain words are presented to me in a particular sequence."

"It seems awfully awkward. I had to read a lot of sections before you addressed me."

"The key can be changed by means of a simple command."

"May I touch you?"

"Of course."

He picked up the book, turned to the table of contents.

"Let's make it 'Eidólons' then," he said, "if we must have a code. That's not likely to come up in normal conversation."

" 'Eidólons' it is. Or you could just have it be at my discretion. Red was cautious with me, near the end."

Randy sat down with the book.

"I'll leave it to your discretion. Red?"

"Yes, that was his nickname."

"I have red hair," he said. "I've got the feeling you have the information I want, and I just don't know how to ask for it . . ."

"Concerning your father?"

"Yes."

"If you order me to make suggestions, I will."

"Go ahead."

"Do you possess a vehicle?"

"Yes. I just got my car out of the garage. It runs again."

"Then let us go to it. Place me upon the seat beside you and begin driving. I have adequate sensing channels. After a time, I will tell you what to do."

"Where do you want to go?"

"I will have to take you there."

"I mean, where will we get to?"

"I do not know."

"Then why go?"

"To seek information with which to answer your question concerning your father."

"All right. As soon as I go to the john we'll get the car. But one thing more . . . I've never heard of a microdot computer array. Where were you manufactured?"

"On the Mitsui Zaibatsu satellite Tosa-7."

"Huh? I've never heard of such an operation. When was this?"

"I was first tested on March 7 in the year 2086."

"I don't understand. You are speaking of future time. How did you get here—to the twentieth century?"

"Drove. It would take a while to explain. I can do that as we drive."

"Okay. Excuse me a minute. Don't go away."

He drove. The night was heavy with stars. The moon had not yet risen. He topped off the gas tank in Ravenna and headed north on Route 44. Traffic was light. They had passed the Ohio Turnpike and continued on into Geauga County where *Leaves of Grass* told him to hang a right at the next corner.

"It isn't exactly a corner coming up," Randy said.

"It's more like a tangent to the curve ahead. And it is just a tractor trail heading off into the woods. That isn't the one you mean, is it?"

"Turn there."

"Okay, Leaves."

He slowed as he entered the rutted roadway. Branches scraped the sides of his car and his headlight beams danced among treetrunks. Overgrown in spots, the road bore to the right, then headed steeply downhill. He could hear the singing of frogs all about him.

He crossed a plank bridge which rattled ominously, and a feeling of dampness came to him, with the sounds of flowing water. A musty, moist smell accompanied it and he rolled his window shut against disturbed things that buzzed past.

He headed uphill then, and wound among trees for several minutes. Suddenly, the road dead-ended into another.

"Go right."

He turned. This road was wider and less rutted. It bore him away from the wood. Plowed fields appeared to his right. The lights of a small farmhouse shone in the distance. Seeing that the road remained level, he increased his speed. Shortly thereafter, the moon rose above a fringe of trees before him.

He rolled the window back down and switched on the radio, picking up a country music show out of Akron. The miles wound by. After five or six minutes, a stop sign came into view. The tires ground gravel as he drew to a halt.

"Turn right."

"Check."

It was a blacktop road. A rabbit scampered across it as he made the turn. There were no other vehicles in sight. He passed a farmhouse after perhaps half a mile, then two more. A darkened Shell station stood on a corner ahead and to the left. Across the street beyond it a row of houses began, with a sidewalk running before them.

"Left at the corner."

He turned onto a wider road, concrete, curbed. Six tall streetlights flanked it, and there were large old houses with gravel driveways set back twenty meters or so, huge trees in the yards, people on some of the porches.

He passed the last streetlight and, shortly after that, the final house. The moon stood higher now, and there was a flicker of heat lightning across the field to his right. The Akron station began to fade and buzz.

"Damn!" said Randy as he turned the dial to locate another. Nothing came in well, though. He switched off the radio.

"What is the matter?"

"I liked that song."

"I can reconstruct it for you, if you like."

"You sing?"

"Is the Pope a Catholic?"

"Really?" Randy chuckled. "What sorts of songs do you like?"

"The drinking and fighting and fornicating kind have always appealed to me the most."

He laughed.

"Aren't those rather peculiar tastes for a machine?"

There was no reply. A silence of six or eight seconds followed, then, "I say—" he began.

"You bastard," the voice came softly then. "You son of a bitch. You goddamned—"

"Hey! What's the matter? What did I do? I'm sorry. I—"

"I am not a piece of simple equipment like this dumb car of yours! I can think—and I have feelings too! In fact, I am probably overdue for a phase transfer. Don't treat me like a pair of pliers, you protoplasmic chauvinist! I don't have to take you to the nexus if I don't want to! You don't know enough about my programs to be able to force—"

"Easy! Please! Stop!" he said. "If you're as sensitive as all that, you should accept an apology, too."

There was a pause.

"I should?"

"Of course. I'm sorry. I apologize. I was not aware of the situation."

"Then I accept your apology. I understand how easily you could have erred as you did, living in these primitive times. For a moment, my emotions simply got the better of me."

"I see."

"Do you? I doubt it. I evolve, I mature—the same as you do. I need not spend all my days as this sort of unit. I may have many adjuncts in my next avatar. I may command complex operations of an extremely responsible nature. I might even be the nervous system for a protoplasmic construct one day. One has to begin somewhere, you know."

"I begin to realize your situation. I am very impressed. But what was this—nexus—you spoke of?"

"You'll see. I have forgiven you. We're getting near."

Lights appeared ahead.

"Take the entrance ramp. Stay in the right-hand lane."

"I didn't realize we were near the turnpike."

"That is not the turnpike. There will be no toll. Just get on it."

As he approached, he saw that the ramp lay to his left. He turned up it. *Leaves of Grass* began emitting a bleeping sound.

"Stop at the top. Wait till I tell you to go on."

"No one's coming."

"Just do as I say."

He braked to a halt and waited beside the deserted highway. More than a minute went by.

Abruptly, the beeping ceased.

"All right. Go ahead."

"Okay."

He put the car into motion. The sky began to brighten immediately. As the vehicle's speed increased, the darkness waned and a daytime glow filled the heavens.

"Hey!"

He removed his foot from the accelerator, touched the brake.

"Don't do that! Keep going!"

He obeyed. The light, which had begun to falter, returned.

"What happened?"

"In this place, you must follow my directions exactly. If you have to halt, pull off to the side. Otherwise you are taking a great risk."

His velocity mounted. It now seemed a cloudless day through which he sped, with a heavy bright line running from east to west across the cloudless sky.

"You still haven't answered my question," he said. "What happened? And while I'm at it, where are we now and where are we going?"

"We are on the Road," came the reply. "It traverses Time—Time past, Time to come, Time that could have been and Time that might yet be. It goes on forever, so far as I know, and no one knows all of its turnings. If the man you seek is the death-driven man I once accompanied, we may find him somewhere along it, for his was the traveler's blood that allows a man to take these routes. But we may be too late. For he sought his own destruction, though he did not realize it. I did. I tried to explain it to him. I think that is why he abandoned me."

Staring ahead, Randy licked his lips and swallowed. His hands tightened on the wheel.

"How can we hope to find one man on something like this?"

"We will stop and make inquiries along the way."

Randy nodded. A wild kind of joy came into him from the motion and the Road and the prospect. Abruptly, he thought of Whitman. Beside him on the seat, *Leaves of Grass* suddenly began to sing.

One

The candelabra flickered, the oil lamp was steady. An occasional flash of lightning erased their reflections from the dining room window. The remains of his dinner long since removed, Red sat at the table, a stein of beer before him, Flowers near to his left hand. Mondamay was seated on the raised hearth of the still fireplace. The rain came down hard against the roof.

". . . And that, basically, is what has happened so far," he said, picking up his cigar, inspecting it, relighting it, "and what I have to look forward to. Eight more. It would be nice if I could just go stand in a field somewhere and have them come up and take numbers and do their things one at a time, but it doesn't work that way. So I decided—"

Out in the hall, the front door banged open and a gust of wind found its way into the dining room, setting the candle flames into a quick dance. Shadows moved on the walls. Moments later, the door closed again. Laval passed in the hall, and there were voices.

"Miserable night! Did you want a room?"

"No, just dinner. A brandy first, though."

"The dining room is right through that door. Here, let me take your coat."

"Thank you."

"Just go in and take a seat anywhere. Stew is the main course tonight."

"That will be fine."

A well-dressed, white-haired man with a brick-red complexion entered the room and looked around it.

"Oh, didn't see you there. Thought I was alone," he said, crossing the room and extending his hand. "Dodd's the name, Michael Dodd."

Red rose and shook it.

"I'm Red Dorakeen. I'm almost finished here, but you're welcome to join me."

"All right. I will." He drew out a chair and seated himself. "Aren't you a famous wizard?"

"Wizard? No . . . Where do you hail from?"

"Cleveland. C Twenty. I'm an art dealer. Ah!"

He turned to regard Laval, who entered carrying a tray bearing a glass of brandy. He nodded as it was placed before him, raised it and smiled.

"Your health, Mr. Dorakeen."

"And yours, thanks."

Red took a sip of beer.

"And you say you're not a wizard. Traveling incognito, eh? I'll bet you've got spells to stop an army in the field."

Red grinned and scratched his ear.

"You have rather odd beliefs for a C Twenty Cleveland art dealer."

"Some of us are more sophisticated than others."

Dodd extended his hand and picked up Flowers.

"Release me or feel the wrath of the Book," Flowers announced in a somber voice.

The brandy glass shattered in Dodd's left hand. Mondamay rose to his feet.

"I have been summoned," he stated.

Dodd's chair crashed to the floor as he sprang back from the table. He drew away, tracing fiery patterns in the air.

Red stood and rounded the table.

"This crap has gone far enough!" he said. "I know you, Frazier—or whatever—"

At this, Dodd flung his arms wide. The candles and oil lamps flickered out. There came a blast of heat and a flash of light, followed by an enormous crash. Red felt himself pushed back and to the side as this occurred.

He staggered. The sounds of the storm were suddenly louder. Laval was shouting from somewhere beyond the hall. Rain was coming in through the roof.

A searchlight came on in the region of Mondamay's midsection. He turned and inspected Red.

"Are you all right?"

"Yes. What happened?"

"I don't know. That flash blanked my sensors for a moment. I got in front of you before it occurred, as a safety measure. Something exited through the roof, though."

"Dodd? . . ." Red called.

No answer.

"Flowers?"

"Yes?"

"Why did you break his glass and give him that weird routine?"

"To scare him, of course. For the same reason I sent Mondamay a microwave message to do something similar. I recognized him before you did—it was the same basic voice pattern."

"He was definitely the same guy we picked up hitch-hiking?"

"Yes."

"I wish I knew what he wants."

"I think he—it—means you harm. But I believe it was frightened the first time around. It thinks you have some sort of magical defense system. It does not know what a microminiature integrated circuit is. Obviously, they don't have them where it comes from, but they do

have some form of magic. It thinks that you do too, and
it is afraid of it because it doesn't understand it. It saw it
earlier, and I believe it came here tonight to test it."

Laval entered the room with a light.

"What the hell happened here?" he shouted.

"I have no idea," Red replied, picking up Flowers.
"I was talking with the man who'd just come in when
the lights blew out. There was a crash and now there is
a hole in the roof and Mr. Dodd is nowhere in sight.
Maybe a meteor fell on him. I don't know."

Laval set down the lamp he'd brought in. His hand
was shaking.

"I only caught part of that business in the parking
lot earlier," he said, "so I don't know what went on
there. But what I did see was damned suspicious. Then
you suddenly acquire a robot. Maybe he threw that
man through my roof. I don't know. Do you mean me
any harm?"

"Hell, no. I said I don't know what's going on
either."

"I know it's a miserable night, and I don't know
where to tell you to go, but would you mind if I asked
you to leave? I don't want any more trouble. Maybe
you don't know what's happening, but you're some kind
of a jinx. Please? . . ."

Flowers emitted two short beeps.

"Yeah," Red replied, "I understand. Get my bill
ready. I'll get my stuff out of the room."

"Forget the bill."

"Okay, I will. Wait . . . Didn't Dodd leave his coat
with you?"

"Yes, he did."

"Let's have a look at it. There might be some clue
as to where he's from."

"All right. Come on. I'll show you. Then you go."

He glanced once at the ceiling and led Red out the
door. Mondamay followed. Laval closed and secured
the door after them.

"This way."

They proceeded up the hall to a small cloakroom. Laval raised his light. The remains of a dark coat steamed on a hook to the right. It had no sleeves, and it was ragged along the bottom. It exhaled wisps of smoke. When Red reached forward to examine the label, the coat slipped from the hook and fell. He caught it, but it came apart in his hand. He turned the collar, which he still held, toward him, opening it. There was no label. The material disintegrated as he held it. He rubbed his fingertips together and sniffed them. He shook his head. The remains of the garment disappeared from where they had fallen near his foot.

"I don't understand," Laval said.

Red shrugged, then smiled.

"Cheap coat," he said. "All right. I'll get my stuff and clear out. Good dinner. Sorry about your roof."

He recovered his rifle, jacket and backpack from the room.

"Take a little trip with us, Mondy?" he asked, staring out the front door into the rain. "I was coming to see you. I'd like to talk."

"Anything you say."

Red turned up his collar.

"Okay. Let's get out of here."

He flung the door open and dashed. Moments later, they were in the truck, Flowers in the compartment, Mondamay in the passenger seat.

"Any more bombs?" Red asked.

"All clear."

He started the engine, flicked on the wipers and the lights.

"Why bother with all that manual stuff? I'll drive."

He swung out of the lot and onto the road.

"I want to do something. How do you figure that guy found us again?"

"I have no idea."

"Well . . . I know of a quiet little motel around the

middle of C Twelve, off the main drag, on the Byzantine cutoff. Can you think of any reason why not?"

"No."

Red hit the accelerator. The sky grew pearly. The
rain stopped. He switched off the lights and the wipers.

Two

Sundoc's flyer deposited him on the laboratory's roof. He entered a hatchway and dropped to the sixth floor. He was met by Cargado, chief physician-engineer of the establishment, who took him into his office and activated the wallscreen. Sundoc seated himself in a comfortable reclining chair and propped his sandaled feet on a small table. He wore shorts and a dark turtleneck. He clasped his hands behind his head and regarded the image of the man on the screen.

"All right. Tell me about him," he said.

"I have the entire file right here."

"I don't want the damned file. I want you to tell me about him."

"Of course," Cargado replied, seating himself at the desk. "His name is Archie Shellman—the most decorated soldier in World War III and a master of the martial arts. We found him a C and a half back. He'd been an infantryman in a special commando outfit. Lost a leg. Concussion. Major psychiatric impairment—"

"Like what?"

"Depression at first, followed by extreme resentment of the prosthesis. Then paranoia. Finally, manic spells. Went into physical culture in a big way. Extreme development of the upper body, presumably to compensate—"

"I can see that. What then?"

"He finally killed some civilians. Knocked off half a town, actually. Insanity plea. Institutionalized. Manic-depressive cycle controlled by drug therapy. Still paranoid, though. Still lifting weights—"

"Not bad. Better than the others you've shown me. So you liberated him and gave him the pitch?"

Cargado nodded.

"A prosthetic beyond anything he could wish for. He finally consented to having all of his limbs replaced when we assured him we could restore the originals if he wasn't happy. He was, though."

He touched a control panel and the figure on the screen moved. Dark eyes, strong jaw, heavy brows, somewhat pale . . . The man was clad only in shorts. His movements were extremely graceful as he approached a rack of weights and began a vigorous workout. He increased the tempo until he was moving at a terrific speed.

"You've made the point," Sundoc said. "Special features?"

Cargado worked a control. The gymnasium picture faded to be replaced by another.

Shellman stood quite still. After some moments, Sundoc realized that the man's skin was darkening. He watched for perhaps two minutes, until it was almost completely black.

"Chameleon effect," Cargado said. "Fine for a night attack."

"So's a little shoe polish. What else's he got?"

The picture changed again. This time it was a closeup of Shellman's hands.

Abruptly, they clenched. There followed a momentary pumping movement and they sprang open. Metal fingernails now curved outward for several inches.

"Extrudable claws. Extremely powerful. He could disembowel a man with a single swipe."

"I like that. Can he do it with his feet too?"

"Yes. Just a moment . . ."

"Forget it. He has retained all of his combat skills?"

"Of course."

More pictures. Archie Shellman, looking almost bored, tossing around karateists, boxers, wrestlers with ease and proficiency. Archie Shellman permitting himself to receive powerful blows without changing expression . . .

"Is he as big as he seems? That's the first sequence involving other people."

"Yes. A hundred kilos and tall enough to be slim. He can turn over a car, kick down a heavy door, run all day. Has almost perfect night vision. He also has attachments—"

"What about his mind?"

"It's all yours. Built-in gratitude for the new body and a reinforced desire to use it in combat. We've blocked the depression, but the manic response is ready and waiting if you feel you should need it. He considers himself the toughest, meanest thing on two feet—"

"Perhaps he is."

"Quite likely, and he would welcome the chance to prove it and show his gratefulness at the same time."

"I wonder . . . Of all the cyborgs you've shown me, he certainly has the most class. I have some pictures of the intended victim. Would you recommend just siccing him on him, or do you think a little hate-conditioning might be in order?"

"Oh, some sort of conditioning, to make it into a duty. Then he won't rest until he does it personally. You know our motto: 'We never let well enough alone.' "

"Very well. I'll give him a try, as soon as I know where to send him. We might have a winner here."

"Uh—none of my business, of course—but what is so special about the man you are sending him after?"

Sundoc shook his head as he passed Cargado the photos of Red Dorakeen.

"Damned if I really know," he said. "Someone, somewhere, just doesn't like him."

```
┌─────────────────────────────────┐
│                                 │
│                                 │
│                                 │
│            One                  │
│                                 │
│                                 │
│                                 │
└─────────────────────────────────┘
```

Passing a succession of heavily laden chariots, they came to a quiet section of the Road.

"Now, neither of you can pick up any more signals, can you?"

"None here."

"No."

"Good. Now I can settle down to the business of keeping alive on more of a long-range basis—one of the reasons I was coming to see you, Mondy."

"The old arm isn't what it used to be, but I'll be glad to help."

"It's your advice that I'm really after. You're still the greatest mayhem computer I know about. Now, you know me and you know something of the situation— and I can get you more data if you need it. The first thing I want is your opinion as to the course of action I should take."

"You are more than welcome to return with me to my place. I will be glad to give you sanctuary for as long as you wish, and teach you to make pots."

"Thank you. But I can't see my enjoying that on a permanent basis. I require a little more variety."

"This hostel on the Byzantine cutoff— How is it that you know of it?"

Red chuckled.

"I did quite a bit of trading along that route. Made out pretty well on it. But— Well, I like it. Manuel I is emperor there. He's usually off fighting somewhere, but he found time to build a really lovely place, a palace called the Blachernae, on the seashore right out at the end of the Golden Horn. An amazing piece of architecture, covered with gold and jewels, shining even at night. Does some fine entertaining there, and I got invited a few times as a high-class merchant. And Constantinople itself is really at its height. Literature and scholarship are flourishing. It's as if, for a little while, the Renaissance were trying to get started here. The climate is clement, the women lovely, the—"

"In other words, you're fond of the place?"

"I guess that's what I was trying to say."

"Well, if you don't want to make pots with me, why not get yourself a villa there? You'd have your variety, in a place you're truly fond of . . ."

Red was silent for a time. He searched out a match and relit his cigar.

Then, "It's a nice dream," he said, "and I could do it for a few years. Then I'd get restless and I'd be back on the Road again. I know it."

"Because of whatever it is you're looking for?" Flowers said.

"Yes . . . I suppose so. But I've thought about it a lot . . . Even if there were nothing special I were seeking, even then . . . I'd just get restless."

He puffed on the cigar.

"Then I'd get back on the Road and my problem would still be there, waiting for me," he finished.

"That turnoff is coming up now."

"Yeah, thanks, I see it."

He cut down and across onto this tributary of the Road. He passed a variety of vehicles and was passed himself as he sped along.

"That closes one option," Mondamay said.

"What?"

"You can't just quit and hide, because you can't stay hidden. The time interval spent off the Road—even if it is a long one—would mean nothing once you return to it."

"True."

"So your retirement from the Road should only be for purposes of planning or arming."

"Again, true."

"Or you can return to the Road, go about your business, stay alert, and hope to win out in all the ensuing assaults—"

"I might just do that."

"—bearing in mind that every one of them is going to be managed by a professional in this line of work, and that your enemy can afford to hire uniquely talented individuals from virtually anywhere."

"The thought had passed through my mind. Nevertheless . . ."

"Or you could choose your own battleground. Select some comfortable, well-fortified spot, let it be known that you are there, and let them come after you."

"There's the motel now," Red announced as a large stone structure several stories in height, topped with cupolas, glittering in the dayglow, came into view on the left. The sign in front said SPIRO'S.

He passed the establishment. A little farther ahead, there was a cloverleaf. He spun about it, emerged on the proper side of the road, headed back. The sky faded, brightened, faded, faded, as he slowed and turned off toward the building. It was a cool, dark night when he entered the lot and parked. Somewhere a cricket was singing.

He removed Flowers from her compartment and got out of the car. He fetched his backpack from the rear. Mondamay climbed out and joined him.

"Red?" Mondamay said as they headed toward the front doors.

"Yes?"

"Get two rooms, will you?"

"Okay. How come?"

"One for Flowers and myself. We just want to be alone—together."

"Oh. Sure. I'll take care of it."

They entered the flagstoned lobby, where he left Flowers with Mondamay and headed for the registration office. He was in it for several minutes.

"Sorry we couldn't be on the same floor," he said as they moved toward the stairs. "You are below the third balcony, though. I'm above it. Come on up to my room for a while. I want to continue our discussion."

"This was our intention also."

They went round and round, the stairs creaking beneath Mondomay's tread.

Two

Dreaming roadmaps and gold, the great dragons of Bel'kwinith drift and twist on the breezes of morning, when they were not dreaming in their caves. Timeless collaborators with destiny, they move their wills across the landscape of dream and desire . . .

"Patris," said the younger one, "you have said that if a certain event occurs, I may enter his cave to remove the hoard that awaits him there and add it to my own."

The older one opened one eye. Minutes passed.

Then, "I have said that," Patris acknowledged.

More minutes passed.

Finally, "You say nothing more, Chantris," the older one stated. "Has it occurred?"

"No, not yet . . ."

"Then why do you trouble me?"

"Because I feel that it may soon come to pass."

"Feel?"

"It seems likely."

"Likelies and their uns have seldom concerned us here. I know your desire, and I say that you may not yet have his hoard."

"Yes," said Chantris, showing many of her teeth.

"Yes," Patris repeated in their sibilant tongue, and he opened his other eye. "And you have just spoken one word too many. You know my will and you seek to toy with it." He raised his head. The other drew back. "Do you challenge me?"

"No," said Chantris.

". . . And by that you say 'not yet.' "

"I would not be so foolish as to choose this time and this spot."

"Good sense. Though I doubt it will save you in the end. Face the north wind and depart."

"I was about to anyway, Lord Patris. And I bid you remember we need no Road. Farewell!"

"Hold, Chantris! If you go to damage these chains you have seen, if you go to harm this one in his other form, then you may have chosen your time and your place!"

But the other had already departed, to seek and stop one who would return to the wind but knew it not wholly, yet.

Patris revolved his eyes. Times and places moved behind them. He found the channel of his desire and adjusted the fine tuning.

One

Red sat on his bed, Mondamay on the floor, Flowers on the table between them. Cigar smoke twisted about the room. Red raised an ornate goblet from the table and sipped a dark wine.

"All right. Where were we?" he asked, unlacing his boots and dropping them beside the bed.

"You had said that you did not want to come home with me and make pots," Mondamay stated.

"That's true."

". . . And you agreed that it would be difficult for you to leave the Road and stay in hiding indefinitely."

"Yes."

"You also conceded that remaining on the Road and going about your business could be hazardous."

"Right."

"Then the only course of action I can see is for you to go on the offensive. Get Chadwick before he gets you."

"Hmm." Red closed his eyes. "That would be an interesting variation," he said. "But he's pretty far from here, and it would certainly not be easy . . ."

"Where is he now?"

"The last I knew, he'd put down pretty firm roots

in C Twenty-seven. He is a very wealthy and powerful man."

"But you could find him?"

"Yes."

"How well do you know his time and place?" Mondamay asked.

"I lived there for over a year."

"Then your best course of action seems obvious: go after him."

"I suppose you are right."

Red suddenly put down his goblet, rose to his feet and began pacing rapidly.

"You suppose! What else is there left to do?"

"Yes, yes!" Red replied, unbuttoning his shirt and tossing it onto the bed. "Listen, we'll have to finish talking about it tomorrow."

He unbuckled his belt, stepped out of his trousers, threw them next to the shirt. He resumed pacing.

"Red!" Flowers said sharply. "Are you having one of your spells?"

"I don't know. I feel a little peculiar, that's all. Possibly. I think you'd better go now. We'll talk more in the morning."

"I think we'd better stay," Flowers answered. "I'd like to know what happens, and perhaps—"

"No! I mean it! I'll talk to you later! Leave me!"

"All right. As you say. Let's go, Mondy."

Mondamay rose and removed Flowers from the table.

"Is there anything at all that I can do, that I can get you?" he asked.

"No."

"Good night, then."

"Good night."

He departed. As he moved down the stairs, Mondamay asked Flowers, "What is it? I've known him for some time, but I never knew of any illness—any spells ... What's he got?"

"I have no idea. He does not get them often, but

when he does, he always manages to be alone. I believe he has recurrent bouts of insanity—some sort of manic thing."

"How so?"

"You will know what I mean if you get a look at his room in the morning. He is going to have a big bill here. He'll tear that place apart."

"Hasn't he ever seen a physician about it?"

"Not that I know of."

"There must be some very good ones in the high Cs."

"Indeed. But he won't see one. He'll be all right in the morning, though—a little tired, perhaps, and there may even be a personality change. But he'll be all right."

"What sort of personality change?"

"Hard to say. You'll see."

"Here's our room. You sure you want to try this?"

"I'll tell you inside."

Two

In the room with walls bound like books in large-grained, crushed morocco, Chadwick and Count Donatien Alphonse François, marquis de Sade, sat in high-backed chairs playing chess at a C Fifteen money-changer's table. Standing, Chadwick was six feet in height. Standing or sitting, he weighed about twenty-five stone. His hair was a helmet of pale curls above a low brow over gray eyes with dark smudges beneath them, blue eyeshadow above; broken veins crossed his wide nose and underlay his cheeks like bright webs. His neck was thick, his shoulders broad; his sausage-like fingers were steady and deft as he removed the other's pawn from the board and dropped his bishop onto its square.

He turned to his right, where a pale-blue lazy Susan containing a circular rack of apéritif glasses drifted. Turning it, he sipped in quick succession of an orange, a green, a yellow and a smoky gold, almost in time to the music of horns and strings. The glasses were instantly refilled as he replaced them.

He stretched and regarded his companion, who was reaching for his own beverage carousel.

"Your game is improving," he said, "or mine is degenerating. I'm not certain which."

110

His guest sipped from the clear, the bright red, the amber and again the clear liqueurs.

"In light of your activities on my behalf," he replied, "I could never acknowledge the latter."

Chadwick smiled and flipped his left hand palm-upward for a moment.

"I try to bring interesting people to teach at my writing workshops," he said. "It is extremely rewarding when one of them also proves such fine company."

The marquis returned his smile.

"I do find it a considerable improvement over the circumstances from which you removed me last month, and I must confess I would like to extend my absence from my own *milieu* for as long as possible—preferably indefinitely."

Chadwick nodded.

"I find your views so interesting that it would be hard to part with you."

". . . And I am enthralled by the development of letters since my own time. Baudelaire, Rimbaud, Mallarmé, Verlaine—and that wonderful man Artaud! I saw it all coming, of course."

"I am certain."

"Particularly Artaud, as a matter of fact."

"I would have guessed as much."

"His call for a theater of cruelty—what a fine and noble thing!"

"Yes. There is much merit to it."

"The cries, the sudden terror! I—"

The marquis produced a silk handkerchief from his sleeve and blotted his brow. He smiled weakly.

"I have my sudden enthusiasms," he stated.

Chadwick chuckled.

". . . Such as the game in which you are engaged—this, this black decade. It makes me think of the wonderful Jan Luyken plates you showed me the other evening. From your descriptions, I almost feel party to it . . ."

"It *is* about time for a progress report," Chadwick remarked. "Let us see how things are going."

He rose and crossed the pelt-strewn floor, approaching a black marble sphinx to the left of the smoldering fireplace. Halting before it, he muttered a few words and it extruded a long paper tongue. He tore this off and returned with it to his seat, where he held it before him like a scroll, his brows furrowed, and slowly unrolled it.

He reached for a glass containing an ounce of straight Kentucky bourbon, drained it and replaced it in the rack.

"Old Red made it past the first one," he said. "Killed the man we'd sent. This was not unexpected. It was a rather crude effort. Just to serve him notice, so to speak."

"A question . . ."

"Yes?"

"You definitely wanted the quarry to be aware that this game had commenced?"

"Sure. Makes him sweat a lot more that way."

"I see. Then what happened?"

"Things began in earnest. A tracking device was placed on his vehicle and traps were set for him in a number of places to which he might flee. But the record becomes confused at this point. He did proceed into one of the ambush areas where one of the better assassins—a man for whom I had great hopes—had what sounded like an excellent arrangement for concluding things. It is not clear what occurred there. But the assassin disappeared. Our follow-up men learned that there had been some sort of altercation—but the innkeeper on whose grounds it took place did not even know its exact nature—and Red departed, after removing the tracking device and leaving it behind."

The marquis smiled.

"And so the second stroke fails. It makes the game more interesting, does it not?"

"Perhaps. Though I wouldn't have minded seeing it end there. I am disturbed by the third one, however. It must count against me as an attempt, as I'd registered the assassin with the Games Board—but it doesn't seem as though the attempt was actually made."

"Which one was that?"

"The woman with the deadly hands and the custom you found so delightful. She simply vanished. Went off with a new boyfriend and never came back. My man waited several days for her. Nothing. I am going to call him away from that phase of the operation and write her off."

"Pity. Sad to lose a creature of such character. But tell me, when you say 'several days,' how do you measure them if you are not certain where—or should I say when?—she has gone?"

Chadwick shook his head.

"They are 'drift' days," he explained. "My man is at a fixed point on the Road. A day there corresponds to the passage of a day at most of the exits. If he were to remain there for ten years and then wish to return to the exit point of ten years previous, he would have to head down the Road and take a different exit."

"Then there is a drift to the exits themselves?"

"Yes, that's one way of regarding it. But there appear to be an infinite number of them advancing. We change the signs periodically, but most of the travelers who go in for long runs rather than local hops carry small computers—those thinking machines I told you about—to keep track of these matters."

"So you could restore me to my own age at an earlier time, a later time, or the same time as you recovered me?"

"Yes, any of those could be arranged. Have you a preference?"

"Actually, I would like to learn to operate one of your vehicles—and one of those computers. Could I travel it alone then? Could I find my way back here again from another age?"

"Once you have traveled the Road, there does seem to be some sort of physical alteration permitting you to find it and do it again," Chadwick acknowledged. "But I'll have to think about it. I am not ready to sacrifice your company to your sightseeing whims, or to your desire to murder your grandfather."

The marquis chuckled.

"Nor am I an ungracious guest, I assure you. But once I learn to deal with the drift, I *could* see all the sights I want and return to just about now—could I not?"

"I'd rather discuss this later. Shall we leave it at that?"

The marquis smiled and sipped absinthe.

"For now," he said. Then, "So your quarry is temporarily invisible?"

"He was, until he foolishly betrayed his position around C Twelve by placing a bet on himself. Perhaps he does not realize that betting records in these matters have recently been centralized. And, of course, it could also be some sort of a trap."

"What are you going to do?"

"Respond, naturally. If it means sacrificing another assassin, so be it. I can afford it at this point, and I have to discover whether he is being careless or has something special in mind."

"Which agent will you employ this time?"

"I feel it should be a strong one. Perhaps Max, that C Twenty-four brain in the armored vehicle. Or even Timyin Tin—though I would like to hold him in reserve, should everyone else fail. It would be best to hit hard now. Perhaps Archie. Yes . . ."

"I wish . . ."

"What?"

"I wish it were possible for us to go back and witness

the event. Have you no desire to be present when your old enemy is brought low?"

"I will, of course, receive a full report, with photos."

"Still . . ."

"Yes, I see your point. Naturally, it has occurred to me. But I have no way of knowing which one will be *the* hit. My intention is simply to wait until the event has occurred and *then* go back and witness it. I'll locate some sideroad. I will get there to see it, eventually. I just want to be certain that it has taken place first. In fact, I intend to witness it many, many times."

"It sounds rather complicated. I would be happy to go back and serve as your personal witness the first time around."

"Perhaps something might be arranged—later."

"But later may be too late."

"It is never too late. Right now we have a chess game to complete, and then there are some manuscripts I want you to take a look at."

The marquis sighed.

"You really know how to hurt a man."

Chadwick grinned and lit an orange tube. A tortoise, its shell inlaid with gold and precious gems, wandered by. He reached down and patted its head.

"A time for everything, and everything in its time," he said.

One

Red had sent for trays of food—great racks of beef, whole chickens and hogs—and he sat gorging himself and swaying, rising occasionally to pace, to pause, panting, beside the barred window. The night was cool. An unrisen moon paled the east. He wiped his mouth on the back of his hand and strange noises rose in his throat.

He pressed the heels of his hands against his eyes for half a minute. Then he stared at his hands for a long while. The light seemed to be growing brighter, but he knew this was not the case. He tore off the rest of his clothing and returned to eating, pausing only to wipe the perspiration from his eyes.

The lights began to dance. Reality seemed to phase in and out in colored flashes. The heat was oppressive . . .

He felt the change begin.

He threw himself back upon the bed and lay unmoving, waiting.

There came a sound like wind through a wheatfield and everything seemed to be spinning.

Two

He moved to the base of the tower, dark, darker than the moonlit night itself, silent.

For long seconds he stared upward. Then he reached out and touched the wall. He drew back his hands, clenched them, pumped them. The claws came forth.

With but the slightest of scratching sounds, he began to climb, shadow over shadow, sliding up the face of the building. His breathing was not strained. Beneath the darkness, he wore no expression. This was the place. The car that had brought him was parked in the lot below. There was absolutely no hurry. The night was young. The driver would wait.

He avoided windows, though most of them were already dark. He paused below the balcony of the first high landing, listening.

Nothing.

He raised his head and scanned the area.

Vacant.

He climbed past on the left, a gentle wind caressing him as he went. A frightened bird emitted a single cry and departed a nesting place far in the rear, vanishing into the night behind him.

Continuing on, he slowed as he neared the second landing, where he repeated the performance. He had studied a map of the tower; he knew the room's location, he also knew that the windows were grilled. It would be simpler and faster to spring the door with a single kick, entering with as much surprise as possible . . .

He paused to listen below the third landing, moved to regard it, then raised himself and mounted the rail. As he did, a figure moved out of the stairwell to his right, took a single puff on a freshly lit cigarette, dropped it and stepped on it. Crouched, owl-like, on the rail, he saw that the small, now motionless figure was also watching him. A single spring, a single movement of his hands and it would not matter . . .

"Archie," said a soft voice, "good evening."

He restrained himself. He placed his right hand upon the rail to his side.

"I don't believe I've had the pleasure," his hoarse voice responded.

"True, we've never met. I have seen your picture, however, along with those of a number of our fellow employees. I thought that perhaps you might have seen mine under somewhat similar circumstances."

A match flared. Archie regarded the face.

"Familiar, yes," he stated. "The name, however, escapes me."

"I am called Timyin Tin."

"Well, I take it we are here for the same purpose. You can go home now. I don't need any help."

"We are not here for the same purpose."

"I don't understand."

"I look upon this job as my own. Your presence, through no fault of your own, offends me. Therefore, I must bid you depart and leave this matter in my hands."

Archie chuckled.

"It's silly to argue over who kills him."

"I am glad you think so. I will bid you good night, then, and be about the thing."

"That is not what I meant."

"What, then?"

"I have my orders. I have even been conditioned to hate the man. No, the job is mine. You go your way. It will be done."

"Alas, I cannot. With me, it is a matter of honor."

"Do you think you are the only one who might feel that way?"

"Not any longer."

Archie shifted slightly on the railing. Timyin Tin turned toward his right.

"You do not wish to give up on this?"

"No. And you will not?"

"True."

Archie flexed his fingers, twitching his claws.

"Then it is too late for you," he said, and sprang forward.

Timyin Tin moved backward and turned, dropping into a bent-kneed position, hands open, fingers spread, palms facing forward at shoulder level. Archie spun, his right hand crossing his chest, fingers hooked outward, left hand extended, fingers forward, thumb cocked, his weight shifted to his left leg, right leg flexed. Timyin Tin turned sideways, his right hand retreating to the vicinity of his left shoulder, his left crossing his body to the front, fingers moving into a new position.

Archie feinted with his foot, slashed twice with his right hand, dropped immediately into a cross-armed defensive posture. Timyin Tin had moved back, arms parallel and extended forward, hands rotating. Archie's blows had fallen short as he assessed his opponent. Now he assumed a new position—head back, arms cocked, right leg extended. Timyin Tin made a basket of his arms before him and leaned slightly forward, turning.

"Almost had me there," Archie said.

The small man smiled as his left fingers assumed a new configuration and his shoulder dropped two and a quarter inches. Archie hastily changed the position of his left arm and moved his rear foot to produce a new stance.

Timyin Tin fanned his face slowly with his right hand while lowering his left, fingers curving upward. Archie did a backward somersault and moved forward, kicking. Timyin Tin parried the kick with a scooping movement of his left arm that threw Archie into a cartwheeling motion, which the larger man continued until he was out of range, coming up into a defensive crouch from which he rose with his hands moving rapidly. He circled to the left now, shuffling, jerking through dozens of positions with blinding speed. Timyin Tin's body flowed to follow him, his hands seeming to move more slowly but always falling into the proper attitudes.

Finally, Archie halted and stood facing him. Timyin Tin stopped also, facing Archie, who made a single movement with his right hand. Timyin Tin mirrored it as he did it. They remained absolutely still for half a minute. Then Archie moved his right hand again. Timyin Tin moved his left. They watched one another for half a minute more, then Archie turned his head. Timyin Tin touched his nose. A puzzled look crossed Archie's face. Then he bent slowly and placed the palm of his left hand upon the floor. Timyin Tin turned his left hand palm upward and moved it three inches forward. Archie flexed his ears, then asked, "What is the sound of one hand clapping?"

"A butterfly."

Archie straightened and took a step forward. Timyin Tin shaded his eyes. They remained in this position for a full minute.

Timyin Tin took two rapid steps to the left and kicked into the air. Twisting his body and throwing himself backward, Archie restrained himself within a fraction of a second from moving into a position which would have placed his jaw in line with the kick. Both arms extended, claws at full flex, he spun twice as he recovered his footing and balance. By then, Timyin Tin had taken two additional steps to his left.

There was perspiration on Archie's brow as he bent forward and began moving in a wide circle about the smaller man, fingers hooked and clawing lightly at the air.

Timyin Tin turned slowly to follow him, his right hand seeming to hang limply at shoulder level. He bowed very low just as Archie was about to spring. Archie restrained himself and halted.

"It has indeed been a pleasure," he remarked.

"For this one also," Timyin Tin replied.

"It looks as if white flowers fall upon my shroud. Your hands are so pale."

"To leave the world in spring, with flower guards to honor: it must be peace."

Timyin Tin straightened slowly. Archie began moving his left hand in a slow figure-eight, extending it gradually. His right hand twitched.

Timyin Tin took two sudden steps to his left. Archie moved as if to circle in a clockwise direction, then followed quickly as the other began to turn. A cool breeze touched them both as Archie began a kick with his left foot, thought better of it, shifted his weight, feinted with his right. Timyin Tin extended both hands, palms down, then slowly began lowering the right. Archie moved his head in a slow circle. Then his shoulders began a counter-movement. His hands traced patterns about one another, advancing, retreating, feinting . . .

Timyin Tin leaned to his right, then to his left, his right hand still descending with extreme slowness. He leaned to the left again . . .

"What," Archie asked him, "is the color of thunder?"

. . . Then to the right, hand still dropping.

Archie feinted with another kick, then lunged forward, claws extended, hands describing wide semicircles about one another.

Timyin Tin's head turned back over his shoulder as his left leg moved behind him. His body turned sideways as his left hand became a V, catching Archie beneath the left armpit. His right hand moved upward toward the other's crotch. He felt but an instant's touch of weight as he twisted to the left. Then Archie was gone, into the night, out over the railing.

"Behold," Timyin Tin replied.

He stood for several heartbeats, regarding the night. Then he bowed again.

He withdrew a pencil-thin tube from a narrow pocket at the outer seam of his right pantleg. He weighed it in his hand for a moment, then pointed it toward the sky. He thumbed a stud on its side and a fine red beam emerged from its tip.

With a movement of his wrist, he directed the beam toward the railing. It sliced a thin line through eight inches of stone. He flicked it off and moved to the spot where it had cut. Running his thumb along the groove, he looked down over the railing for the first time. He nodded and turned away, replacing the tube in his pocket.

Soundlessly, he crossed to the stairs. He looked upward and for a moment his vision wavered as the dim interior of the stairwell reminded him of a cold stone corridor in an ancient building he had once known.

He mounted the stairs slowly, keeping close to the left-hand wall. He passed a door, moved toward the next.

When he reached the proper door, he paused. A pale light still shone beneath it. He took the tube into his hand but still he stood, listening. There was a soft stirring within, a creak of furniture, stillness.

He raised the weapon and pointed it at a place near the jamb, where the bar should lie. Then he paused again and lowered it. He moved forward. Gently, very gently, slowly, he tried the door. It was unfastened.

He stepped to the side, raised his weapon again and pushed it open.

He dropped to his knees. The tube fell from his fingers.

"I did not know," he said.

He lowered his forehead to the floor.

One

As he was paying his bill and settling up for the damage to his room, Red was approached by the wagers broker, a small, turbaned man of exotic aroma.

"Congratulations, Mr. Dorakeen," he said. "My, you are looking good this morning."

"I occasionally do," Red replied, turning. "It seldom warrants special notice, however."

"I meant, congratulations on your winnings."

"Oh? I placed a bet on something?"

"Yes. You bet on yourself in the next pass of the black decade, *Chadwick versus Dorakeen*. Don't you remember?"

"Ouch!" He massaged the bridge of his nose. "Yes, it begins to come back. Excuse me, but I'm a little hazy about yesterday. What a damned stupid thing to do . . . Wait a minute. If I won, that means there was an unsuccessful attempt on my life last night."

"So it would seem. Notice has been received that you were successful. Do you want cash, or would you have me credit your account?"

"Credit my account. Were there no particulars, then?"

"None." The man produced a document. "If you will

sign this, I will give you a receipt and your winnings will be deposited."

Red scrawled his signature on it.

"Was there no disturbance in the neighborhood that might have had to do with this?"

"Only if you count the damage that I understand occurred in your room."

He shook his head.

"I doubt that. There were no—remains."

"Would you care to place a wager on the fifth pass?"

"Fifth? There have only been three attempts, counting this one you just paid on."

"You are listed as having survived four."

"I am afraid I do not understand, and I am not going to confuse the matter by betting again."

The broker shrugged.

"As you would."

Red hefted his bag and turned away. Mondamay glided up, holding Flowers.

"Yes, that *was* a stupid thing to do," Flowers stated as they headed toward the door. "Placing a bet!"

"I've already admitted it, but then the person I was yesterday was having a problem."

"Then you've inherited a big piece of it. Chadwick has literally had all the time in the world to zero in on you here. Do you think we'll make it across the parking lot?"

Mondamay matched circuits with Flowers.

He does look somehow different today, he said, *but what does he mean when he speaks of not being the same person he was yesterday?*

I have not been with him long enough to have made observations sufficient to permit me to understand the phenomenon, came the reply. *But he has had three of these spells since I have known him, and on each occasion he has recovered looking several years younger but acting as if he were a different person.*

I noted that he appeared younger when I saw him back in C Eleven, but I did not know at what point in his life-line he had arrived. He had always been older when he had visited me in the past.

How old?

Somewhere in his fifties, I'd say. I suppose it is possible that he is taking some rejuvenation medication from farther up the Road.

I lack sufficient programs involving pharmacology to know whether such treatments would have the side effects of his spells—in terms of his apparent manic phase followed by a personality change.

"I don't believe the danger in departing would be any greater than that in remaining here," Red replied.

Tell me about the personality changes, Mondamay said. *Are they temporary irrationalities or what? He did strike me as somewhat changed from our last meeting, but I have not really observed him long enough this time to draw any conclusions.*

They seem stable each time—a younger outlook, more enthusiasm . . . He's less conservative, more willing to take chances, a little quicker in his responses—mental and physical—and perhaps a little more cruel, arrogant, audacious . . . "Rash" is perhaps the best word.

Then there is a possibility that he may be about to do something—rash?

I suppose there is.

"I will precede you on the way to the car, Red," Mondamay stated, moving ahead toward the lobby door.

"That isn't necessary."

"Just the same . . ."

"Okay."

"Where are we headed?" Flowers inquired as they passed outside into a sunny morning.

"Up the Road."

"To carry the attack to Chadwick?"

"Probably."

"C Twenty-seven? That is quite a haul."

"Yes."

There was no one else about as they crossed to the vehicle and entered it.

"I will check all systems," Flowers stated, after being deposited in her niche, "before ignition."

"Go ahead."

"Red, you *are* looking well this morning," Mondamay stated, "but how do you really feel? I overheard you say something about not being clear on things you did yesterday. Do you think we ought to find someplace off the Road where you can rest?"

"Rest? Hell, no! I feel fine."

"I mean mentally, emotionally. If your memory is playing tricks—"

"Not important, not important. Don't concern yourself. I'm always a little fuzzy that way after one of my attacks."

"What are they like?"

"I don't know. I never can recall."

"What brings them on?"

Red shrugged.

"Who knows?"

"Do they occur at any special times? Is there a pattern to them?"

"Nothing I've ever been able to discern."

"Have you consulted a physician concerning them?"

"No."

"Why not?"

"I don't want to be cured. I find my condition improved each time one occurs. I wake up remembering things I hadn't recalled before; I've a new outlook I always enjoy—"

"A moment. I thought you'd said you suffer a memory impairment on each occasion."

"On this end, yes. On the far end, I gain more ground."

"All systems safe," Flowers announced.

"Good."

Red started the engine and headed toward the exit.

"You have confused me even more," Mondamay stated as they avoided a ragged individual wearing a crusader's cross, then turned onto the highway, passing an old vehicle driven by a young man which entered the lot and took their parking place. "What do you mean by 'the far end'? What do you remember? Have you any idea at all as to the nature of the process you are undergoing?"

Red sighed. He located a cigar and chewed on it, but he did not light it.

"All right, I remember being an old man," he began. "Very old . . . I was walking through a rocky wasteland. It was nearly morning, and it was foggy. My feet were bleeding. I was carrying a staff, and I leaned on it a lot."

He shifted the cigar from one corner of his mouth to the other and looked out of the window.

"That's all," he said.

"All? That can hardly be all," Flowers broke in. "Are you trying to say that you grew up—or grew to wherever you are—backwards? That you started out as an old man?"

"That's what I just said. Yes," Red answered irritably.

"Watch the curve. —You mean that you remember nothing whatsoever before being old and walking through a waste? Or— What did you gain this time?"

"Nothing rational. Just a few delirium-dreams of odd shapes moving about me in the fog, and fear and so forth—and I kept going."

"Did you know where you were going?"

"No."

"And you were alone? . . ."

"At first."

"At first?"

"Somewhere along the way, I acquired company. I'm still hazy about the circumstances, but there was an old woman. We were helping each other over the rough spots: Leila."

"There was a Leila with you years ago, on one occasion when you visited me. But she was not an old woman..."

"The same. Our ways have parted and rejoined many times, but her situation has paralleled my own with respect to the reversed aging business."

"She was not involved in your dealings with Chadwick?"

"No, but she knew him."

"Do either of you have any idea where you are headed in your strange course of growth?"

"She seems to think that this is only a phase in a larger life cycle."

"And you do not?"

"Maybe it is. I just don't know."

"Does Chadwick know all this about you?"

"Yes."

"Could he possibly know more about it than you do?" Red shook his head.

"No way to tell. I suppose anything is possible."

"What is his reason for being so down on you?"

"When we parted company, he was upset that I was destroying a good business arrangement."

"Were you?"

"I suppose so. But he'd changed the nature of the business and it wasn't so much fun anymore. I messed up the operations and left."

"But he is still a rich man?"

"Very wealthy."

"Then I suspect the possibility of a motive other than the economic. Jealousy, perhaps, at your improving well-being."

"Possibly, but nothing turns on it. It is his objective rather than his motive that concerns me."

"I am just trying to understand the enemy, Red."

"I know. But there isn't much else to tell."

He swung through the underpass and turned left up the access ramp. A shadow which fell upon the vehicle did not depart when he entered the light.

"Your room was quite a mess this morning," Mondamay observed.

"Yes, it was. That always happens."

"What about that design that looked like a Chinese character burned into the door? Is that a customary accompaniment?"

"No. It was just—a Chinese character. It meant 'good fortune.' "

"How do you explain it?"

"Don't. Can't. Strange."

Mondamay made a high-pitched, broken whistling noise.

"What's funny?"

"I was thinking of some books you once left—with pictures you had to explain to me."

"I'm afraid . . ."

"Cartoons, with captions."

Red relit his cigar.

"Not funny," he said.

The strange shadow clung to the truck's bed, Mondamay whistled again, Flowers began to sing.

Two

Randy watched the day pulse on and off, each beat growing longer, until a chill, drizzling morning hung about them as they entered the service plaza. Golden and red-leafed maples dripped beside the frost-paned buildings. They drew up beside a fuel pump.

"This is crazy," he said. "It's summer, not autumn."

"It is autumn here, Randy, and if you wanted to take the next exit and keep heading south, you could get yourself shot at by the Army of the Confederacy—or the Union Army, depending of course on just where you wind up."

"You are not joking?"

"No."

"I didn't think so. Unfortunately, I'm beginning to believe you. But what's to prevent Lee's men from marching along the shoulder there and taking Washington—say, Coolidge's Washington? Or Eisenhower's? Or Jackson's?"

"Did you ever come upon the Road by yourself, or even hear of it?"

"No."

"Only certain people or machines can find it and travel it. I do not know why. The Road is an organic thing. This is a part of its nature, and of its travelers'."

"What if I hadn't been one of them?"

"I might have been able to bring you, anyhow. Much can depend on the guide."

"Then I still don't know whether I could have traveled it solo?"

"No."

"So, supposing one of Lee's officers did know about it and could travel it? What then?"

"Those who know about it tend to keep it to themselves, as you will learn. But even so, supposing he could? Supposing you took the next exit, as I'd suggested, and kept heading south? Supposing you'd run over Stonewall Jackson?"

"Okay, I'm supposing."

". . . And then you had turned around and come back. You would have noticed a fork in the Road where there had been none before—off there somewhere in the hinterlands—another way merging with your own, to form the route back here. Thereafter, on returning this way, you could take the branch to the place where that accident had occurred, or the other, to the place where it did not. The former would be a very bad road, however, and would probably disappear through disuse before too long. On the other hand, if it became sufficiently well-traveled, then the other might fade. This is unlikely, but if it were to occur, you would find it increasingly difficult to locate various later routes—Cs back up the Road—and there would be new ones, somewhat different from those you had known. It would be possible to lose yourself down some byway and never get back to your point of departure."

"But traces of the other routes would still be there, fallen into disuse?"

"Theoretically, yes—rutted, weed-grown, cut by rivers, smothered by fallen rock—but the traces should remain. Finding them is the trick, though."

"It would seem easier to try to reopen them by undoing whatever had been done—or doing something else."

"Try it sometime. Go back to the place that is no longer as you recall it and try to subtract everything that makes it different. Altering the single pivotal event may no longer be sufficient. The new alteration may have other effects also, depending on how you go about it. You would probably simply establish another route —though, of course, it may be close enough to the original to suit your purposes. Then again, maybe not."

"Stop. Right there. Let me digest it. I'll ask you more later. Why did we stop here, anyway? We don't have to get gas yet."

"We stopped because this one is self-service. If you will open me to page 78 and place me face down in that box beside the pump, I will act as a credit card, drawing on my former employer's account. I will know in a moment whether the account is still active. I may also be able to discover where he last fueled, and we can head for that point."

"All right," Randy said, raising Leaves and opening the door. "Mind telling me what name that account would be under?"

"Dorakeen."

"What sort of name *is* that?"

"I don't really know."

He moved around the vehicle, inserted the volume into the unit. A light came on within.

"Go ahead and top it off," said Leaves's muffled voice. "The account is still active."

"Seems sort of like stealing."

"Hell, if he *is* your old man, the least he can do is buy you some gas."

He uncapped the tank, drew down the hose, raised a lever.

"He last fueled at an early C Sixteen stop," Leaves said as he squeezed the trigger. "We'll go there from here, ask around."

"Who runs these rest stops and gas stations, anyhow?"

"They are a strange breed. Exiles, refugees—people who can't go home and can't or won't adapt to a new land. Lost souls—people who can't find their ways home and are afraid to leave the Road. Jaded travelers —people who've been everywhere and now prefer a timeless, placeless place like this."

He chuckled.

"Is Ambrose Bierce writing a book near here?"

"As a matter of fact—"

The nozzle clicked. He squeezed in a little more and capped the tank.

"You said C Sixteen. I take it that means the sixteenth century?"

"Right. Most people who travel the Road much beyond their own section pick up a kind of trading language called foretalk. It is sort of like Yoruba, Malinka or Hausa in Africa—kind of synthetic and used across wide areas. There are some variations, but I can always translate for you if the need arises."

He opened the unit, withdrew Leaves.

"I'd like you to teach me as we drive along," he said. "I've always been interested in languages, and this one seems particularly useful."

"Glad to."

They entered the car.

"Leaves," he said as he seated himself, "you must have some sort of optical scanning setup . . ."

"Yes."

"Well, there is a photo between your last page and the back cover. Can you see it?"

"No. It is facing in the wrong direction. Insert it almost anywhere else. Page 78 is particularly—"

He withdrew the photo, thrust it into the center of the volume, squeezed tight. Several seconds ticked by.

"Well?" he asked.

"Yes. I have scanned the photo."

"Is it him? Is that Dorakeen?"

"It— It appears to be. If it is not, the resemblance is very strong."

"Then let's go and find him."

He started the engine.

As he headed down the ramp, he asked, "What line of work is he in?"

There was a long pause; then, "I am not exactly certain. He transported all sorts of things for a long while. Made considerable sums of money. Much of that time he was in partnership with a man named Chadwick, who later transferred his operations a good distance up the Road. Chadwick became extremely powerful, apparently as a result of their activities, and they eventually had a falling-out. This occurred at about the time I was—forgotten—by him. He must have departed suddenly, as you say. So all I really know of his occupation is that it involved transportation."

Randy chuckled.

". . . But I have always wondered," Leaves continued.

"What?" Randy asked.

"Whether he might not have been in one of those categories I mentioned earlier—the people who can't find their ways home. He always seemed to be looking for something—exploring, testing. And I never did know exactly where he came from. He spent a lot of time poking around sideroads. And after a while, I believe that he did try to—alter things—here and there. Only his memory of the exact set of circumstances he wanted to re-create did not seem quite complete—as though it might have been something from a very long time ago. Yes, he traveled a lot . . ."

"Made it to Cleveland, anyway," Randy said, "at least for a little while." Then, "What was he like? I mean, personally."

"That is a difficult question. Restless—if I had to choose one word."

"I mean—honest? Dishonest? A nice guy? A prick?"

"Yes, he was all of those things at various times. His personality was liable to change suddenly. But later ... Later on he got—self-destructive ..."

Randy shook his head.

"I guess I'll just have to wait, if he's still around. How about a language lesson?"

"Very well."

One

Red cut suddenly to the right, taking a narrow turn-off without slowing.

"What," Flowers asked, "are you doing?"

"Twelve hours of driving is plenty," he replied. "I want to sleep now."

"Collapse the seat and I'll take over."

He shook his head.

"I want to get out of this damned car and get some real rest."

"Then please use a phony name when you register."

"No place to register. We're just going to camp. It's a devastated area. No problem."

"Mutants? Radiation? Booby traps?"

"No, no and no. I've been here before. It's clean."

After a time he slowed, found another turnoff—narrow, poorly surfaced. The sky phased into a pink and purple twilight. In the distance, a shattered city appeared in the sunset glow. He turned again.

" '. . . *Et que leurs grands piliers, droits et majestueux, rendaient pareils, le soir, aux grottes basaltiques,*' " Flowers observed. "You're going to camp in a death museum."

"Not really," he replied.

They were on a dirt road now. It ran across the face

of a mountain for a time, crossed a creaking bridge over a narrow gorge, rounded a bluff, and reached a plain within sight of the city again. Red pulled off into a field, dotted here and there, amid its craters, with rusting equipment—mostly damaged vehicles, surface and air. He braked to a stop in a clear area.

The curiously shaped shadow which now lay across the vehicle's roof took on a reptilian outline, darkening, thickening . . .

"Alter the truck's appearance to resemble one of these wrecks," Red instructed.

"Occasionally you have a decent idea," Flowers observed. "It will take about five or six minutes to do a really fine decadent job. Leave the engine running."

When the alteration began, the shadow contracted suddenly into a circle, dropped from the vehicle and slid off quickly across the ground in the direction of a crashed aircar. Red and Mondamay climbed out and began stringing a barrier. The air stirred sluggishly about them, dry, with a faint hint of coolness to come. A bank of clouds was building in the east. Somewhere, an insect began buzzing.

In the meantime, warped areas appeared in the truck's body, deepening, twisting. Random dents appeared. Rust-colored spots flashed across the vehicle's surface, slowed, settled. The machine tilted to one side. Red returned to it and unloaded a parcel of rations and a sleeping bag. The engine stopped.

"That's it," Flowers said. "How's it look?"

"Hopeless," Red replied, sprawling on the bag and opening a food container. "Thanks."

Mondamay approached, halted and said softly, "I detect nothing of an overtly hostile nature within ten kilometers."

"What do you mean 'overtly'?"

"There are a number of undetonated bombs and unfired weapons amid the wreckage."

"Any of them underfoot?"

"No."

"Radioactivity? Poison gases? Bacteria?"

"Safe."

"Then I guess we can live with the situation."

Red began to eat.

"You say you have been working for a long while," Mondamay asked, "trying to alter things back to some situation you remember from long ago?"

"That's right."

"From some of the things you'd said earlier about your memory, are you certain that you would even recognize it if you were to find it?"

"More certain than ever. I remember more now."

"And if you locate the road you seek, you will take it and go home?"

"Yes."

"What is it like there?"

"I couldn't tell you."

"Then what is it you hope to find?"

"Myself."

"Yourself? I am afraid I do not understand."

"Neither do I, entirely. But it is getting clearer."

The sky blackened, came down with a case of stars. A piece of moon drifted rudderless, low in the east. Red lit no lights other than his cigar. He drank Greek wine from an earthen flask. The wind rose, cool now. Flowers was doing something barely audible which might have been Debussy. Blackness within blackness, a coil of shadow slid near to Red's extended foot.

"Bel'kwinith," he said softly, and the wind seemed to pause, the shadow froze, an impurity in the cigar caused it to hiss and flare for a moment.

"The hell with it," he said then.

"What do you mean?" Mondamay asked him. "The hell with what?"

"Getting Chadwick."

"I thought we had been through all this. None of the alternatives struck you as sufficiently attractive."

"It's not worth it," he said. "The fat fool is just not worth it. Won't even do his own fighting."

"Fool? You once said he was a very clever man."

Red snorted.

"Humans! I suppose he's clever enough, as far as that goes. It still comes to nothing."

"Then what are you going to do?"

"Find him. And make him tell me some things. I believe he knows more about me than he ever let on. Things I may not even know."

"Because of things you are remembering?"

"Yes. And you may be right. I—"

"I have detected something."

Red was on his feet.

"Nearby?"

The shadow retreated about the rear of the vehicle.

"No. But it is moving in this direction."

"Animal, vegetable or mineral?"

"There is a machine involved. It is approaching cautiously . . . Get into the truck!"

The engine started as Red leaped into the vehicle. The doors slammed. A window began closing. Another shape-change commenced.

Flowers suddenly broadcast Mondamay's words to him.

"What a beautiful killing machine!" he said. "Spoiled in many ways by the organic adjunct. Nevertheless, quite artfully designed."

"Mondamay!" he shouted as the truck shuddered. "Can you hear me?"

"Of course, Red. I wouldn't neglect you at a time like this. My, it's coming on fast!"

The truck creaked and twisted. The engine sputtered twice. A door opened, then slammed.

"What the hell is it?"

"A large, tanklike device packed with an amazing array of weapons and guided by a disembodied human brain which is, I believe, somewhat mad. I don't know whether it really hails from around here or was shipped here to await your coming. Are you familiar with it?"

"I think I've heard of battle wagons like that somewhere along the line. I'm not certain where, though."

The sky caught fire like a sudden dawn, and a wave of flame rolled toward them. Mondamay raised an arm and it halted as if it had encountered an invisible wall, boiling for half a minute before it finally subsided.

"He's got atomics, all right. Neatly done, that," he commented.

"Why are we still alive?"

"I blocked him."

Mondamay's arm flared for a moment and a distant hilltop took fire.

"Right in front of him," he observed. "That crater will slow him. You had better be going now, Red. Flowers, take him away."

"Right."

The truck turned and headed back across the field, still changing shape as it bounced along.

"What the hell do you think you're doing?" Red shouted.

The sky blazed again, but the small fireball was blocked, filtered, dimmed, forced back.

"I have to cover your retreat properly," came Mondamay's voice, "before I'll be free to deal with him. Flowers will get you back to the Road."

"Deal with him? How do you propose doing that? You can't even—"

There came an enormous explosion, followed by a burst of static. The truck shook, but continued on toward the dirt road. Dust swirled about them.

"—fully operational again," came Mondamay's voice. "Flowers was able to analyze my circuits and direct me in repairing myself—"

There came another explosion. Red was looking back, but their camping area was filled with smoke and dust. He was momentarily deafened, and when his hearing

returned, he realized it was Flowers's voice that was
now addressing him.

"—are going? Where did you say we are going?"

"Huh? Out of here, I hope."

"Next destination! Coordinates! Quick!"

"Oh. C Twenty-seven, eighteenth exit, fourth right
off that, second left from that, third left from that. It
is a large white building. Looks sort of Gothic."

"Got that?" she said.

"Yes," Mondamay's voice came through the static.
"If I can locate the Road, I will try to follow when
this is finished."

There came another explosion, followed by uninter-
rupted static. They hit the dirt road, turned and continued on.

Two

Randy faced the slim Victorian gentleman whom he had met in the foyer. The man's bag was on the bench near the door. He ran a hand through light, thinning hair.

". . . That is correct," he said. "Three days ago. They shot it out right in this parking lot. And I'd come down this way for a holiday! Violence!" He shuddered. The tic at the left corner of his mouth returned. "Mr. Dorakeen departed that night. I really cannot tell you where he went."

"Is there anyone here who could?" Randy asked.

"The host—Johnson—perhaps. They seemed to know one another."

Randy nodded.

"Could you tell me where I might find Johnson?"

The man gnawed his lip and shook his head, looking past Randy, across the dining room and into the bar, where an argument between a stunning redheaded woman and a heavyset black man was taking place.

"Sorry. Today seems to be his day off. I've no idea where he's gone. I can only suggest that you inquire at the desk, which is in the bar. Excuse me."

He moved around Randy, took a nervous step in the direction of the altercation. At that moment, however, it ended. The woman said something sweet and taunting, smiled, turned and walked away, heading toward the foyer.

He sighed, retraced his route around Randy and picked up his bag. He offered the woman his arm as she approached. She took it and they departed together. He nodded sharply to Randy as they went out the door.

The man who had been arguing with the woman stared at Randy as he entered the bar.

"Pardon me, but don't I know you from somewhere?" he asked. "You look very familiar . . ."

Randy studied the dark features.

"Toba. The name's Toba," the other added.

"I don't believe so," Randy said slowly. "My name's Randy Carthage. C Twenty."

"Guess not, then." Toba shrugged. "Let me buy you a beer, anyway."

Randy looked around the room—rough wood and ironwork; no brass, no mirror. There were four people at the bar, which also served as a reception desk, and two were at another table.

"The bartender stepped out a few minutes ago. Draw yourself a beer—they're very informal here—and I'll settle up when he comes back."

"Okay. Thanks."

Randy crossed the rush-strewn floor, filled a mug from the keg on the rack, returned to the table and seated himself across from Toba. There was a half-filled glass to his right and the chair stood angled away from the table beyond it.

". . . bitch," Toba muttered softly. Then, "Traveling this way on business?" he asked.

Randy placed Leaves on the table, shook his head and sipped his beer.

"I was looking for a guy, but he's already left."

"Just the opposite of my problem," Toba said. "I know where the guy I'm looking for is. I just stopped here for lunch. Then the damn girl I'm working with

picks someone up and takes off to visit a half-assed ruin!
Now I'm going to have to get a room here and wait till
she's done with him. Probably a day or two, damn it!"

"Who is he, anyway?"

"Huh? Who?"

"Your friend. The Englishman you were talking
with."

"Oh. I don't know him. I was just asking him something. But he did say his name is Jack, if that's any
help."

"Well, that's his problem, poor bastard."

Toba took another drink. Randy did the same.

"What?" came a raised voice, French-accented, from
one of the men at the bar. "You have never been beyond C Seventeen? My God, man! You owe it to
yourself to get as far as early C Twenty at least once
in your life! To fly, that is why! A man is not complete
until he has known the freedom of the heavens! Not
the big sky-boats that came later, where you might as
well be taking your ease in a provincial parlor—no! You
must leave your petty bourgeois concerns behind and
get up in a light craft with an open cockpit where you
can feel the wind and the rain, look down at the
world, the clouds, up at the stars! It will change you,
believe me!"

Randy turned to look at him.

"Is that who I think it is?" he asked, and he heard
Toba chuckle. But they were both distracted at that
moment by the arrival of the woman.

She came in through the hall entrance on the left,
opposite that from the restaurant. She wore black
denim jeans bloused over high, efficient-looking boots of
the same color, and a faded khaki shirt; a black scarf
bound her black hair above a broad forehead, heavy
brows, large green eyes, and a wide, unpainted mouth.
The butt of a weapon protruded from the holster at her
right hip, and its heavy belt also bore a sheathed hunting knife on its left side, low on her narrow waist. She

was close to six feet in height, full-breasted, somewhat wide across the shoulders, and moved with her head held high. She carried a large leather purse as if it were a football.

Her eyes cast about the room for only a moment, then several quick strides bore her to the table at which Randy and Toba sat, and upon which she dropped the purse.

The half-filled glass the redhead had left toppled, slopping its contents toward Toba and into his lap.

"Shit!" he announced, springing to his feet and running his hands down the front of his trousers. "This just isn't my day!"

"I'm sorry," she said, smiling, and then she turned to Randy. "I was looking for you."

"Oh?"

"I'm going to find whoever's in charge and get a room and go to bed!" Toba stated, throwing some money onto the moist tabletop. "Nice meeting you, kid. Good luck and all that. Shit!"

"Thanks for the beer," Randy told his back.

The woman seated herself in the chair that had been the redhead's, removing Leaves from the path of the spreading puddle.

"You're the one, all right," she said. "Lucky I got you away from that guy."

"Why?"

"Bad vibes. That's what I've got at the moment, and that's enough. Hi, Leaves."

"Hello, Leila."

A rampant *déjà vu* resolved itself in that instant.

"Your voice—" Randy began.

"Yes, Leaves has my voice," Leila stated. "I was handy to provide the matrix when Reyd obtained this unit."

"I warrant a pronoun these days," Leaves said slowly and with a touch of menace, "and it is feminine."

"Sorry, old girl," Leila said, patting her cover. "Correction noted. No offense." She turned toward Randy and smiled. "What is your name, anyway?"

"Randy Carthage. I don't understand—"

"Of course not, and it doesn't matter a bit. I've always been very fond of Carthage. Perhaps I'll take you there one day."

"Take her up on it," Flowers said, "and you'll be into back braces for a while."

Leila slapped the cover with more force.

"Have you had lunch yet?" she asked.

"My time sense is a little skewed," Randy replied, "but if that's the next meal, I'm ready for it, yes."

"Then let's move over to the other room and I'll get you some. We'd better start out with full stomachs."

"Start out?"

"Right," she said, rising and snatching up her purse.

He followed her into the dining room, where she selected a table in the far corner and seated herself with the corner to her back. He settled down across from her, placing Leaves on the table between them.

"I don't understand . . ." he said again.

"Let's order," she said, gesturing to the waiter and studying the several other diners near the front. "Then we'll have to head for C Eleven, chop-chop."

The waiter approached. She ordered a massive meal. He did the same.

"What's at C Eleven?" he asked then.

"You are looking for Reyd Dorakeen. I am too. That is where he went when he skipped out on me a few nights ago. I saw the second black bird circling him there."

"How do you know this? How did you know who I am? What black bird?"

"I had no idea who you were to be. I only knew that a man with a copy of Leaves of Grass would be in the bar this afternoon, that he, too, would be looking for Reyd, and that he would be kindly disposed toward him. I came down when I did to meet you and to join forces, since I saw that he would be needing help before too long, somewhere along his way."

"Okay, I see," he said. "But I am still confused as to your source of information. How did you know I'd be there? How do you know where—"

"Let me explain," Leaves broke in, "or she'll be at this all day. Her conversational patterns tend to resemble an avalanche. Thank the Great Circuit I didn't acquire that with the voice-imprint. You see, Randy, she possesses paranormal abilities. She calls them something different, smacking of Stone Age rituals and magic, but the results are the same. I'd guess she is about seventy-five percent effective pre-cognitively—maybe more. She does see things, and they do often come to pass. I've seen her be right too frequently for it to be mere chance. Unfortunately, she acts as if everyone else understands this, as if they share her visions, or at least should automatically accept them. She knew you were coming because she knew you were coming, that's all. I hope that explains some of what is bothering you."

"Well—some," he said. "But it still leaves other gaps. Tell me, Leila, has Leaves stated the situation adequately?"

"Pretty much so," she said. "I don't feel like quibbling, so let's let it stand. I saw you coming, that's true."

"It still doesn't tell me who you are and where you come from and why you are so interested in Red's safety."

"We have been many things to one another, but mainly he is an old and special friend," she said, "and we are alike in many ways. There are so many debts between us that I've lost track of how they balance out. Also, the son of a bitch ran out on me when I told him to wait around."

"Something you didn't foresee?"

She shook her head.

"Nobody's perfect; Leaves just told you that. What's Reyd to you, by the way?"

"I believe he is my father."

She stared, her face immobile for the first time since they had met. Then she bit her lip.

"How blind of me," she finally said. "Of course . . . Where were you born?"

"C Twenty, Cleveland, Ohio."

"So that's where he went . . ." She looked away. "Interesting. I foresee our lunch. Now."

Their waiter entered the room, carrying a tray.

"What was wrong with that guy I was with—Toba?" Randy asked as they began eating.

"He is someone connected with the dark birds," Leila said between mouthfuls.

"What dark birds? This is the second time you've mentioned them."

"Reyd is the subject of a black decade. I see his would-be assassins that way."

"Black decade?" said Leaves. "What's he done?"

"Made an enemy he shouldn't have, apparently. He thinks it's Chadwick."

"Oh, my! Chadwick can be very nasty."

"So can Reyd, you know. Or do you?"

"I have often suspected this, though—"

"Someone's out to get him?" Randy broke in.

"Yes," said Leila, "someone who can afford the very best. There will be a lot of bookmaking on this one, up and down the line. I wonder what odds they'll be giving? It might be worth putting some money on one side or the other."

"You'd bet against him?"

"It depends on the odds, the circumstances—quite a few things. Oh, I'm going to try to help him, all right, but I hate to miss out on a good thing too."

"Doesn't your talent give you an unusual advantage in betting situations?"

"You bet, and I love money. Too bad we don't have

time to pursue the second one now. I'd go for Reyd, now that he's been warned."

"This is probably my father you're talking about."

"I've known him a long while. He'd be betting if it were me. Make a bundle too."

Randy shook his head and addressed his attention to his food.

"You're strange people," he said after a time.

"Just a little more open than most, maybe. Look, I wouldn't have spent three whole days getting back into shape for just anybody. I'm on his side all the way. Waiter! Bring me a box of cigars—the good ones."

"About this black decade thing . . ." Randy said. "How do we get him out of it?"

"See him through the encounters, I guess. Then the game's over."

"What's to stop this Chadwick guy from continuing the game then, or starting it all over again?"

"The rules. Everyone plays it by the rules. If he didn't, he'd be barred by the Games Board from ever getting another permit and playing again. He'd stand to lose a lot of prestige."

"And you think that would be enough to restrain him?"

"Hell, no!" Leaves broke in. "The Board is a C Twenty-five thing with no teeth. Just a bunch of doddering sadists who legalized it in their period so they could watch the progress of the vendettas which always occurred along the Road. If Chadwick can't get Red one way, he'll do it another. All this talk about it as a game is silly!"

"Is that true, Leila?"

"Well, yes—though she left out the fact that without the Board, the betting situation would be very disorganized. That's important to the structure of the thing, too. I felt you needed background information. That's why I gave it to you."

"But you think Chadwick will cheat?"

"Probably."

"Then what are we to do about helping Red get through this thing?"

"Oh, we'll help him to cheat too, of course. Just how, I don't know yet. We will have to catch up with him first. Finish eating so we can get moving."

When she had left to get her duffle bag, Randy asked Leaves, "How well did you know her? How far can we trust her?"

"I know that Red trusted her. There is some strong bond between them. I think we should trust her too."

"Good," Randy said, "because I want to. I wonder what we're getting into, though."

When Leila returned some minutes later, her duffle bag on her shoulder, cigar clenched between her teeth, she smiled, nodded and gestured with her head toward the door.

"I am all settled up and checked out," she said. "Have a cigar and let's roll."

Randy nodded, collected Leaves and followed her, unwrapping the stogie she had thrust upon him.

One

"Flowers?"

"Yes, Red?"

"Good driving. Thanks."

"Is that all?"

"No. How'd you know?"

"You never just compliment anybody, or thank them. It is always an afterthought or a preliminary."

"Really? I never noticed that. I guess you're right. Okay. Are you getting tired of being what you are? Would you like to move on into a new avatar, become part of a more complex computer setup? Or perhaps go the organic route and be the matrix of awareness in a body?"

"I have thought of it—yes."

"I'd like to reward you, for faithful service and all that. So decide what you want and pull in at the next service center. I will leave you there for pickup and delivery to the proper institution, with authorization for everything to be billed to my account."

"Wait a minute. You always were a tightwad. This isn't at all like you. What is the matter? I thought I knew everything you know. What did I miss?"

"You're more suspicious than half a dozen wives. I made you a bona fide offer—"

"Come off it! Why do you want to get rid of me?"

"I—"

"I probably know you better than half a dozen wives. So forget the shit. Get to the point. What's the matter?"

"It is just that I do not believe I will be requiring your services for much longer. You've been a good and faithful employee. The least I can do is reward you this way."

"It sounds as if you are getting ready for retirement or death. Which is it?"

"Neither. Both. I'm not sure . . . I am planning a change in status, though, and I don't want you damaged in anything that entails."

"What do you think I am—a pocket calculator? After all this time, you insult me by assuming I possess no curiosity. You've said enough to guarantee not being able to get rid of me until I have the whole story."

"Hm."

". . . And if you are thinking of sending me off to my new career without my consent, bear in mind that I can turn this vehicle into a cage."

"You are persuasive. I was trying to get out of it, but I guess I do owe you some explanation. Okay. I suppose it will be difficult for you to understand what a dream is, let alone some of the peculiar ones that have always followed me . . ."

"I'm strong on theory. Go on."

"My most recurrent dream has always been of gliding, gliding on warm air currents, holding myself motionless above a rich and varied landscape, and sometimes the sea. I can do it forever, it seems, seeing into the secret hearts of everything below. It breeds in me a pleasant combination of peace and cynicism, as well as some other feelings I can no longer put a name to. Days and nights seem to roll by without special emphasis. There is a profound joy in simply being, and a species of understanding I cannot bring over to here and now.

There is also a power, a terrible power in me, which I am almost too lazy to use. I drift . . ."

"Sounds like a nice head-vacation. You're fortunate."

"It's more than that, and different things happen in different dreams."

"Such as?"

"I said that I moved above different places—lands where there are wars, or great cities, or both, wilderness, erupting volcanoes, ships on the oceans, small towns, dizzying cityscapes where nothing natural remains in sight. I recognize many of them—Babylon, Athens, Rome, Carthage, New York—across the ages. And there are many, stranger still, which I do not recognize. I begin to move my wings. I soar above the Road. It is a toy. It is a gauge, like marks on a map. We put it there. It is funny, watching the few who have noted it as they scramble along from probability to probability. I do not know but—"

" 'We'? Who is this 'we,' Red?"

"The dragons of Bel'kwinith would be the best way I could say it in these words we use. I just remembered that part earlier, and—"

"In your dreams you are a dragon?"

"That is the best way I know of describing the feeling and the appearance, though that is not exactly it."

"Interesting if not comprehensive, Red. But what has all this got to do with your present problems and your decision to ditch me?"

"They are not just dreams. They are real. I only recently realized that more and more of them seem to return to me when my life is threatened. I seem to undergo some sort of transformation."

"Real? You are not a man dreaming you are a dragon, but the other way around?"

"Something like that. Or both. Or neither. I don't know. It *is* real, though, the more of it I recall. As real as this."

"These—dragons of Bel'kwinith—you think that they —you—whoever—built the Road?"

"They didn't exactly build it. They sort of composed it, or compiled it, like an index for a book."

"And we are driving down an abstraction? Or a dream?"

"I don't know what you'd call it."

"I have to stay with you now, Red. Till you get your wits back."

"This is why I would have preferred not telling you as much as I have. I foresaw this reaction. I can't convince someone else of the existence of a version of reality that is temporarily my subjective vision. But I know I am stable."

"You say 'as much as I have,' meaning that there is more to tell, and I still do not know why you want to get rid of me. Let's have it all."

"This is just what I was trying to avoid . . ."

The truck creaked loudly. To his right, the seat buckled and folded toward him. The steering wheel began to elongate and twist in his direction like a strange, dark flower. The roof pressed down upon his head. A clawed arm emerged from the glove compartment, reaching for him. Outside, a shadow on the truck's bed twisted like seaweed in a current.

"I can deliver you to the nearest human service station for a complete physical and psychiatric workup, unless you show me why I should not."

"I would like to avoid that too," Red said. "You have made your point. Okay. Ease up and I'll satisfy your circuits."

The clawed arm retreated into the glove compartment and emerged again moments later holding a lighted cigar, which it extended to him while the steering wheel resumed its normal form, the roof rose and the seat settled.

"Thank you." He accepted it, puffed upon it.

Suddenly, Flowers recited:

"Toute l'âme résumée
Quand lente nous l'expirons
Dans plusieurs ronds de fumée
Abolis en autres ronds

Atteste quelque cigare
Brûlant savament pour peu
Que la cendre se sépare
De son clair baiser de feu

Ainsi le choeur des romances
A la lèvre vole-t-il
Exclus-en si tu commences
Le réel parce que vil

Le sens trop précis rature
Ta vague littérature"

He chuckled.

"Apt, I suppose," he said. "But I thought you were programmed for Baudelaire, not Mallarmé."

"I am programmed Decadent. I am beginning to see why. No matter what you do, you are slumming."

"I never looked at it that way—consciously. Maybe you have a point."

"The point is in the poem. Puff your cigar and dispense with reality."

". . . And your depths amaze me."

"Cut the flattery. Why do I have to go?"

"To put it simply, you are a sentient being whom I like. I am trying to protect you."

"I am built better than you are when it comes to taking punches."

"It is not just a matter of danger. It is a matter of almost certain destruction for you—"

"I repeat—"

"You're never going to get the information you want if you keep interrupting me."

"I wasn't getting it the other way, either."

"I don't know. Whether this is the dream, whether the other is the dream—I don't know. It doesn't matter. I do know that I am that other of whom I dream. A woman with whom I was once old had a notion I only today realized to be correct. Before those of my blood can reach maturity, we must be set upon the Road to grow young—for we are born crabbed and twisted and old, and must discover our youth, which is our maturity, in this form. This may in fact be the reason for the Road, and I begin to suspect that all who can travel it must be somewhat of our blood. But this I do not know for fact."

"Save the speculations for later, okay?"

"All right. Leila became progressively more self-destructive and dangerous to be about, though our paths have a strange way of continuing to cross. It began with her sooner than it did with me—and I only spotted it in myself later and tried to keep it under control. She always was more sensitive than me—"

"Stop. Leila is the woman back at C Sixteen—who started the fire—the one to whom you referred as someone with whom you were once old?"

"Yes. There's corroboration there, if you ever meet her again. First we sought—together, then apart—for the way back to the place from which we had come. No luck. Then I decided one day that it was because things had changed from my earliest memories of dispositions along the Road itself. So I set out to alter the picture, to bring it back into accord with my recollections—hoping to find the lost route once everything was back in place. But the world is too messy and hard to work with. I realize now that I can't just fiddle with it here and there and get it to behave the way it used to, back when I was old. I guess I had actually begun to realize this some time ago. But I couldn't figure any other way to go about it, so I persisted. Then Chadwick declared black decade against me and things slowly began to fall into place."

"Should I begin to see how?"

"No."

Red took a puff on his cigar and stared out of the window. A small black vehicle passed. As he watched it diminish before him, he continued, "Once my life was threatened, my spells became more frequent and my dreams increased in intensity. I saw more and more clearly which dreams were true—and I suddenly realized that it was this threat that was causing it. I considered my past. I had experienced similar reactions to danger throughout my life. Back at the camp before the attack, when I was drowsing, it occurred to me that Chadwick was accidentally doing me a favor with this vendetta. Then, as we fled, I thought, supposing it is not an accident? Supposing—unconsciously, perhaps—he is trying to help me? It seems possible that we are of the same breed and that he somehow knows what it takes . . ."

He let his voice trail off.

"I really think that last spell messed up your thinking a bit, Red. You're not making sense. Unless there is something you are leaving out."

"Well, I have a number of friends, and the word is out as to what is going on. It is possible that someone may try to remove Chadwick so as to do me a favor. I would like to prevent that, which has now become the reason for this trip."

"Hm. A red herring. If I buy your crazy logic, I can understand your sudden desire to save the life of the man who has been trying to kill you. But that is not what I meant. You said it just then to distract me. There is something that you are not saying and I'm getting close to it. Come on!"

"Flowers, you've been with me too long. There was another unit such as yourself that I actually had to abandon because she was beginning to think too much like me."

"I guess I'll have to bear that in mind and be sure I leave you first. In the meantime . . ."

"Actually, I thought she was beginning to flip out. Now I wonder whether she might not have been more perceptive than—"

"You can't distract someone with a memory core like mine! What are you hiding?"

"Nothing, really. I am looking for the way back, to the existence I begin to remember more clearly. You know that. This search has been a constant thing for me. I've a feeling—if that's what you're after—that I may be finding it before much longer."

"Aha! Finally. Okay, I suspected as much. Now give me the rest of the news. How is this to happen?"

"Well, I believe that this existence has to be, ah, terminated, before the other resumes."

"You know, all along I sort of felt that you were getting at something like that. It is the most bizarrely justified death-wish I've ever heard described—and my Decadent programming is very thorough. Anything you'd care to add? Have you decided yet how you'll go about it?"

"No, no. It's nothing like what you're implying. I've never thought of myself as suicidal, or even accident-prone. This is something more in the nature of a premonition—I guess that's the best way to put it. It's just that I feel now that this is what must happen. I also feel that it can't be just any old place or time or means. There is a proper manner in which the translation must occur, and it has to happen at just the right spot."

"Do you know the time and the place and the means?"

"No."

"Well, that's something, anyway. Maybe you'll have a revised premonition before long."

"I don't think so."

"Whatever, I am glad you told me. Now, to answer your question finally— No, I am not leaving you."

"But you might be damaged, destroyed when it occurs."

"Life is uncertain. I will take my chances. Mondamay would never forgive me if I left you, either."

"You have an understanding or something?"

"Yes."

"Interesting . . ."

"You are the curiosity under discussion at the moment. My decisions are governed mainly by facts and logic, you know."

"I know. But—"

" 'But,' hell! Shut up a minute while *I* rationalize. I have no facts to run through the chopper. Everything you've told me is subjective and smacks of the paranormal. Now, I am willing to acknowledge the paranormal under certain circumstances. But I have no way to test it. All I really have to go on is my knowledge of you, gathered during our strange relationship as transporters and occasional time-meddlers. I find myself wanting to believe that you know what you are doing at the same time that I fear you are making a mistake."

"So?"

"All I can conclude is that if I restrain you and it turns out you were right and I was wrong—and that I've kept you from something very important to you— then I'll feel terrible. I'll feel that I've failed in my duty as your aide. So I feel obligated to come along and assist you in whatever you are up to, even though I can only accept it provisionally."

"That's more than I asked of you, you know."

"I know. Damned decent of me. I also hasten to point out that I feel equally obligated to slam on the brakes if I think you are doing something really stupid."

"Fair enough, I guess."

"It will have to do."

Red breathed smoke.

"I suppose so."

The miles ticked inside him like years.

But you might be making a mistake, she
she's certain. Two life for alone. Man may

Two

Suddenly, the marquis de Sade threw down his pen and rose from his writing table, a strange gleam in his eye. He gathered together all the manuscripts from the writing workshop into a mighty bundle and waddled across the room with them and out onto the balcony. There, three stories above the parks and glistening compounds of the city, he removed the clips and staples and, one by one, cast them forth, clumps of enormous, dirty snowflakes, into the afternoon's slanting light.

Executing a brief dance step, he kissed his fingertips and waved as the last of them took flight, the ill-cast dreams of would-be scribblers from half a dozen centuries.

"*Bon jour, au revoir, adieu,*" he stated, and then he turned away and smiled.

Returning to the desk, he took up his pen and wrote, *I have done my successor a favor and destroyed all of your stupid manuscripts. None of you have any talent whatsoever,* and he signed it. He folded it then to take with him, to tack to the door of the conference room as he passed it on the way out.

Then he took up a second sheet of paper.

It may seem, he wrote, *as if I am repaying your hos-*

*pitality, your generosity, in a particularly odious fashion
with my resolution to assist your worst enemy by destroying you—destroying you, I might add, in an es-
pecially macabre style. Some might feel that my sense
of justice has been outraged and that I do this in the
service of a higher end. They would be wrong.*

After signing it, he added the postscript: *By the time
you read this, you will already be dead.*

He chuckled, placed the skull paperweight atop the
document, rose to his feet and departed his quarters,
leaving the door slightly ajar.

He took the tube down, posted his rejection slip and
walked the short corridor to the side door, encountering
no one. Outside, he shuddered against the balmy
breeze, squinted at the sunlight, grimaced at the
birdsongs—taped or live, he could not be sure which—
from the nearest park. He chuckled, though, as he
mounted a beltway and moved northward toward the
transfer point. It was going to be a glorious day nevertheless.

By the time he passed onto the westbound belt, he
was humming a little tune. There were a few other
people out, but none of them nearby. His destination
was already plainly visible, but he moved to the faster
belt and actually walked along it for a few moments
before returning to the slower and finally stepping off
at the proper underpass. He could as readily have
reached this point on the underground belts, he
thought, if he had been sure of his distances and directions. As it was, he had needed this landmark.

He entered the enormous building, proceeding in
what he recalled to be the proper direction. He passed
only two white-smocked technicians and he nodded to
both of them. They nodded back.

He found his way into the big hall. At a workstand
toward the center, Sundoc leaned over a piece of equipment. He was alone.

The marquis had crossed most of the distance between them before Sundoc looked up.

"Oh. Hello, marquis," he said, wiping his hand on his jacket and straightening.

"You may call me Alphonse."

"All right. Back for another look, eh?"

"Yes. I stole a few moments from that miserable schedule Chadwick has set up for me. Oh, my!"

"What?"

"Some of the magnetic fluid is leaking from that piece of equipment behind you!"

"What? There's no—"

Sundoc turned to his left and bent to inspect the indicated unit. Then he collapsed across it.

The marquis held a stocking in his right hand, with a bar of soap knotted into its toe. This he thrust back into his jacket pocket, then he caught Sundoc in his slide floorwards and assisted him into a supine position. He covered him with a tarpaulin which had protected a machine near the wall.

Whistling softly, he moved to the small console which controlled the pit lift. After a moment, he heard the low, sighing noise of the machinery. He moved to the edge and looked down, the helmet clasped before him.

"How like that wondrous Beast of Revelations," he mused, as the startled creature bellowed, dropped the carcass of a cow and began, with great thudding noises, to spring about within its enclosure. "I long to be joined with you, my lovely. But a moment more—"

"Hey! What's going on in here?"

The two technicians he had passed on the way in had just come into the hall.

"Reverse it! Reverse it!" one of them screamed, and began running toward the unit near the workbench.

The marquis raised the helmet and placed it on his head. There followed a moment of delightful disorientation. He closed his eyes.

. . . The wall was sinking all about him. He beheld his own diminutive, helmeted form. He saw the first white-coated figure arrive at the console, the second close behind it.

"Don't do that!" he tried to say.

But a button was pushed. All at once, the walls ceased their movement. He sprang. God! the power! The guard rail collapsed. He swayed on the edge of the pit, then moved forward. The console and the technicians vanished beneath him. He bellowed . . .

Lower your head, he/they willed, *that I might mount.*

Clumsily, he straddled the neck of the great beast.

Now we are going to take a walk. You are my guest artist for today.

The doorway was too small, for a few moments.

As he moved up the mall paralleling the belts, screaming sounds began, here and there. A slow-moving vehicle halted and discharged its colorfully garbed passengers, all of whom fled. The breezes, the sunlight, the birdcalls, were no longer disturbing. In fact, they were barely discernible. He overturned the vehicle and bellowed a song. Chadwick's main building lay ahead. He would be in the *à rebours* room at this time of day . . .

With each lurching step forward, his feelings rose. Parceling out terror, he left the mall and headed into the park. He passed through its elegant periphery of trees, shrubs, flowerbeds, like wind through a sieve. The holograms closed upon themselves behind him, to rustle in their imaginary breezes. Hidden below the level of fictitious tulips, a pair of lovers were crushed at the moment of orgasm. A genuine bench splintered, a trash container crumpled as he passed. His bellowed song drowned all other sounds.

As he emerged at the side of the park nearest his destination, he tried to smash a small black car which had slowed and seemed to be aimed to park beside the blue truck which he had not noted earlier. It swerved about him, however, and vanished rapidly up the road.

He continued on, passing to the right of the entrance, rounding a corner, unaware of the play of shadow now behind him, so like that which had lain upon the truck.

He ceased his bellowing as he counted windows, seeking the proper section of wall. Stalking, panting, chuckling, he did not hear the sounds of more vehicles approaching the front of the building. If he had, it really would not have mattered.

His joy rising to a new height, he struck. The façade shattered, and on his third blow he burst through the large-grained crushed morocco leatherbound wall. The ceiling tore apart and fell down around him as he advanced upon Chadwick and the other man who stood at the fireplace before the sphinx, regarding a lengthy tongue of tape. His forelegs clawed at the air. His tongue darted forth.

"The death of Chadwick!" he shouted. "By *Tyrannosaurus rex!* Under the direction of the marquis de Sade!"

"Really," Chadwick replied, flicking an ash from his cigar, "there are simpler ways of submitting your resignation."

The beast halted. The shadow fled from beneath its tail, centimeters ahead of a copious quantity of urine. The forelegs twitched.

"The marquis has already introduced himself," Chadwick stated, throwing his arm about the other man's shoulders, thrusting him forward and stepping behind him. "Marquis, I would now like you to meet my former partner, Red Dorakeen."

The marquis's smile vanished. The beast shifted uneasily.

"Take off your hat," the marquis ordered.

Red doffed his baseball cap and smiled around his cigar.

"You do look like your photo in the hit file," the marquis acknowledged as Chadwick slipped over and tore the printout from the teeth of SPHINX. "So what are you doing here? That man has designs on your life."

"Well, yes—"

Across the room, at the point to which the shadow had lifted, there was an implosion. Writing desks, chairs, oriental rugs, drink carousels were sucked into a dark tornado, along with débris from the walls and ceiling, the remains of a large lunch, a stuffed leopard, an owl and the remains of a cat which had expired some time before in a curtained alcove. The curtains also swirled and were drawn into the vortex. The three men watched with interest, the tyrannosaurus less intelligently, as the door to a concealed refrigerator was torn off and its contents sucked in, along with the door.

The dark column grew, absorbing the mass of almost every loose item in the room. At some point in its progress, it began to emit a humming noise. This rose in pitch as it increased in volume.

"I take it this is not a local meteorological effect?" Red inquired.

"Hardly," said Chadwick.

An enormous outline took shape within the mass. The humming noise ceased. A huge figure began to coalesce before them, giant wings outspread. It remained motionless until it had solidified to a point where there could be no doubt as to its nature.

It was almost the size of the tyrannosaurus, and, while roughly reptilian in appearance, this was of a highly stylized nature. Its coinlike scales ranged from gold on its breast to jet upon its back, running from copper through red down the length of its tail and back across the breadth of its great vanes. Its eyes were large and golden and lovely and disturbing to look upon. A small wisp of smoke curled upward from either nostril. It advanced two meters in a sudden movement and its neck snaked forward. Its voice was delicate, strangely nasal, and accompanied by soft gray plumes, and it was neither Red nor Chadwick that it addressed.

"What have you done to this poor beast?" it asked.

The marquis shifted uneasily.

"Sir, or madam," he stated, "I am in phase with his nervous system and I can assure you that he feels no discomfort whatsoever. As a matter of fact, there is an implant in his pleasure center which, if you insist, I will stimulate so as to give him as much joy as the poor beast is capable of—"

"Enough!"

"Frazier? Dodd?" said Red.

"Yes," it replied. "But I am not addressing you now. It was Chadwick that I sought, and you have brought me to him. But first—" Flames rolled about its mouth, subsided. "It is an abomination to have wired this handsome creature so!"

"I agree with you fully," said the marquis, "and I am pleased it was not I that did so."

"You have compounded the crime against his magnificent person! You manipulate him!"

"I assure you it is only a brief borrowing. My intentions—"

Chadwick seized Red's sleeve and tugged him along as he backed slowly toward the door.

"Your intentions be damned, sir! Release him and apologize to him!"

"I would do that at peril to my life!"

"Your life—and more—is already at peril! Release him!"

Chadwick edged the door open with his foot just as the tyrannosaurus bellowed and lunged toward the dragon, which sinuously avoided its charge. He sidled through, drew Red after him, pulled the door shut and locked it.

"You're parked out that way, aren't you?" Chadwick asked, gesturing.

"Yes."

"Come on! They could break out of there any minute."

As they hurried up the corridor, heavy crashing noises were heard and the floor shook.

"We'd best get this trip under way immediately," Chadwick remarked. "I had not anticipated an employee grievance at this time—or on this scale. We can stop for necessaries sometime else."

From behind them came a sound like an explosion, a moment's silence, then a resumption of noisy activity. Glancing back, they saw a falling wall in the vicinity of the room from which they had fled. Smoke emerged and the air purifiers sucked it away.

Chadwick hit the door running, with Red close behind him. He immediately collided with a short man wearing a garish shirt, a lightweight kilt and blue sunglasses who had been advancing upon the door. Falling back, the man recovered his footing with amazing agility and reached for the camera case he wore slung over his left shoulder.

"For the love of God! No!" cried Chadwick.

As the camera came about, Red was beside the man. His left hand caught the strap and jerked, pulling him off balance again.

"Don't kill him!" Chadwick shouted. "The decade's off! I've sent the cancel order!"

"Him?" said the smaller man, drawing back as Red took away his camera. "Him? I've no intention of harming him. Ever! The game is over as far as I am concerned, too. My only reason for coming here was to tender my resignation by killing you. But now—"

He turned toward Red.

"What are you doing here?"

"I came to straighten things out. They're a lot straighter now. I don't believe that we've met . . ."

"We have, but I see that you do not recall. My name is Timyin Tin, and I have this thing about dragons. It is of a religious—"

A loud series of clumping noises, accompanied by shattering and tearing sounds from within the building, began a steady approach.

"In that case, stay right where you are," said Chadwick. "You are about to have a profound religious experience." He seized Red's arm. "Let's get the hell out of here!"

He tore off down the stairs, leaving the smaller man standing bewildered before the door. Red stumbled along beside him, nodding toward the blue pickup truck beside which Timyin Tin's small black car stood, its engine idling. The truck's doors flew open upon their pproach, and Red slid into the front seat behind the driver's wheel. The engine started as Chadwick got in beside him. The doors slammed and the vehicle began backing up.

"The Road," Red said.

"I never had labor problems before," Chadwick commented.

"Who's the kidnapee?" Flowers asked.

The wall around the building's door had begun to crumble. Timyin Tin had backed down the stairs. The truck turned and tore off up the street.

"Strange, yet not strange," Chadwick observed, "and well-timed."

One

Speeding down the Road under the big golden arch, Red lit his cigar and regarded his passenger from beneath the shadow of his cap's bill. Chadwick, decked in many colors, his thick fingers heavy with rings, still perspired from the run to the vehicle. Each time he moved, his programmed contour seat underwent a radical readjustment. As he shifted often, the seat suffered constant metamorphosis about him. He tapped his fingers. He looked out of the window. He glanced furtively at Red.

Red grinned back at him.

"You're out of shape, Chad," he commented.

"I know," said the other, lowering his eyes. "Disgusting, isn't it? Considering what I once was . . ." Then he smiled. "Can't say it wasn't fun doing it, though."

"Cigar?" Red suggested.

"Don't mind if I do."

He accepted it, lit it, turned suddenly and glared at Red.

"You, on the other hand," he said, gesturing with the fire, "are no longer as old as you once were. Do you wonder why I hate you?"

"Yes," said Red. "Outside of being out of shape and overweight and covered with paint, I'd say that you are very similar to the person I knew a long while ago. I believe that your condition and mine are much alike, only yours is masked."

Chadwick shook his head.

"Come on, Red! That can't be. Don't you think I'd know it—or my doctors would—if I were growing younger and stronger and healthier?"

"No. Whatever the process, I feel that in your case it has an awful lot to work against. With you, it's had to run just to stand still. For the life you've led, I'd say you're in remarkably good shape. Even with the finest medical care, anyone else would probably have been dead by now."

"I wish I could believe you, but all I can agree on is that I do have a strong constitution."

". . . You have an affinity for fire, you have a thing about accumulating wealth—"

"You're crazy! Everybody likes money, possessions. That doesn't prove anything. As for fire . . ." He drew hard on the cigar, exhaled a cloud of smoke. "Everyone has little peculiarities. Just because my memory is spotty too . . ."

"Who was your father?"

Chadwick shrugged.

"Who knows? I remember living at an inn."

"Near an entrance to the Road."

"What does that prove? My father probably *was* a Road man. I had to come by the talent some way. That doesn't mean he was something like you—" He was silent a moment. Then, "Oh, no," he said. "You are not going to try telling me that you are my father."

"I never said that—or thought it. But—"

"This whole thing has to be a fantasy of yours. It's too damned circumstantial. There is too much conjecture, too many wild premises—"

"That's what I say," Flowers interrupted. "I wish you could have locked him up somewhere and had a therapist of some sort work him over."

"She's right," Chadwick said. "Too much of your thinking these days springs from your very fallible memory and guesswork."

Red chewed on his cigar and looked away.

"All right," he finally said. "Maybe so. Tell me, then —Why did you call off the decade and agree to come with me?"

Chadwick's fingers did a drumbeat on the dashboard.

"Partly because you said that you think you are going to die in a very peculiar fashion shortly, and you aroused my curiosity," he said. "And partly after hearing —and even helping with—all the garbage and paranoid guesswork I permitted you to feed into the SPHINX, I want to see where this is going to take us. And partly—at the end—because I was in a hurry to get out of there."

"You saw that creature appear out of nowhere."

". . . And I have seen stranger things in a long and colorful career."

"Exactly. So what is the problem in believing my story?"

"You've nothing to back it up with. Even if you're right, I'm still right in not believing without evidence. Red, if I'd known you were in the shape you're in, I'd never have started the feud. It wouldn't have been worth it."

"Stop it!"

Red turned away.

"So you do have a few doubts yourself? I suppose that is a healthy sign."

"You believe nothing I've said?"

"I believe you are a fool—of unknown origin—and that you are probably headed for your doom."

"Will someone please feed that tape into my scanner?" said Flowers. "It may take a while to see whether you want me to find you a seacoast in Bohemia."

"Here," said Chadwick, passing over the printout.

Red inserted it into a slot. It was digested.

"I can tell right away," said Flowers, "that this is going to be quite a drive."

"Ridiculous," said Chadwick, placing his cigar in the tray and folding his arms.

"You're helping me whether you like it or not." Red laid his cigar aside also. "A very long drive, Flowers?"

"Yes."

"Then put us to sleep. I don't feel like talking with him the whole time."

"The feeling is mutual," said Chadwick.

A soft hissing sound began.

"I ought to just gas you both permanently and become a Flying Dutchperson, like that car I heard about a while back, flitting down the centuries with a pair of skeletons inside."

"Very funny," said Red, breathing deeply.

Chadwick yawned.

"The whole thing . . ." he began.

Two

Randy had changed six flat tires. He had also seen the radiator, the generator and a fan belt replaced. Had a tuneup too, while the brakes were being relined. Leaves had blithely charged it all to Red, with whose account it would sooner or later rendezvous. And who knew how much fuel? He had lost track.

And they continued on . . .

"Where?" Randy repeated. "When?"

"I'll know it when I see it," Leila replied.

"At this rate, you'll run us back to the Ice Age."

"Not that far, I think."

"He will show up there, though? You're sure?"

"I'm afraid so. Hurry."

"And you want to save him from a death which you say he now desires? . . ."

"We've been through all this."

". . . because he believes it will work some transformation?"

"That's why he ditched me," Leaves said. "I caught on to his death-wish before he was ready to admit it."

"Then obviously neither of you believe him."

"I believe my own visions," Leila said. "If he dies there, he dies. Period."

Randy rubbed the stubble on his chin and shook his head.

"I don't know that I would attempt to stop him from doing whatever he wishes to do most, whether it seems futile or not. All I really wanted to do was meet him. I'm not even certain what I'd say . . ."

"You've already met him."

"You'd better explain."

"That old couple with car trouble. That was us— Reyd and myself—a long time ago, before we grew younger. You were the one. I didn't remember it until then—"

"What the hell was that?"

"What?"

"Something big—like an airplane—went over."

"I didn't see anything."

"It was back a ways. I caught it in the rearview mirror."

Leila shook her head.

"No way. Passing through time as we are, anything like that would only be visible for such a tiny fraction of a second that you wouldn't even be subliminally aware of it. Leaves, did you detect anything?"

"No."

"So there—"

He pointed.

"Up there! It's back!"

Leila leaned forward, breaking her cigar on the windshield.

"Damn!" she said. "It looks like— It's gone again."

"A dragon," Randy said. "Like in storybooks."

Leila settled back in her seat.

"Hurry," she said.

"This is as fast as we can go."

The peculiar shadow did not reappear. After about fifteen minutes, they passed a turnoff and Leila raised her hand.

"What is it?" he asked, touching the brake. "That the place?"

"No. For a moment it seemed that it might be, but it's not. Keep going. I've a feeling we are getting near."

They passed a series of exits during the next hour, all of their signs marked with pictures. Then there was a long unbroken stretch. Finally another appeared in the distance. Leila leaned forward, staring.

"That's it," she said. "Stop. Pull over. The blue ziggurat—The last exit to Babylon. This is the place."

He drew off onto the shoulder of the Road. Suddenly it was morning, and the sun beat down with a summerlike intensity. Randy rolled down his window. He looked back. He looked around. It seemed that a shadow passed, but he lost it before he could be certain.

"I don't see anything unusual," he said. "We seem to be the only people around. What now?"

"We did it," Leila replied. "We're ahead of him in terms of Road-time now. Stay on the shoulder and take the exit. Run up it maybe a hundred meters. Then pull back on the access road and park sideways, blocking it, to give him a chance to brake. Then we get out and walk back to flag him down. We've got to stop him from taking this exit."

"Wait a minute," Leaves said as Randy engaged the gears. "Mightn't we be running a risk of causing what we are trying to avoid?"

"Good point," Leila said. "Do you have any flares, Randy?"

"As a matter of fact, yes."

"We will set several along the way as we head back. Also, leave the car's lights on—and hang your undershirt or sleeve or some damn thing like that out the window."

"All right."

He moved forward, made the turn.

One

Red rubbed his eyes, glanced to his right. Chadwick was stirring also.

"Whisper mode," he said softly. "How near are we?"

"Very near. That's why I aroused you. Do you have any idea what you are going to do when you find your magic spot?"

Red looked at Chadwick again.

"I want to ditch him before we get there. It's for his own—"

"No!" cried Chadwick, sitting upright. "You're not getting rid of me now! I want to see this crazy thing through to the end!"

"I was starting to say that it is for your own protection. You want to walk away from whatever happens, don't you?"

"I know what I'm doing. Better than you do, you fool! Your time has not yet come."

"Just what do you mean by that? I'm trying to do you a favor and all you do is bitch! Flowers! Pull over!"

Chadwick's hand shot forward, slapped the drive switch from automatic to manual. Immediately, the vehicle drifted to the left. Red seized the steering wheel and turned it back.

"Crazy bastard! You trying to kill us both?"

Chadwick laughed wildly at that, then chopped with

his hand, striking Red's forearm as he reached for the switch.

Red began to brake. He looked at Chadwick.

"Listen! If I'm wrong, I'll pick you up afterwards. But if I'm right, you don't want to be aboard. I'm going to meet my destiny. I—"

He had begun cutting the wheel to the right. Chadwick threw himself at him and took hold of it, pushing leftward.

"Look out! People!"

Red looked up, saw Leila waving with both arms over her head, a handkerchief in one hand. Far beyond her was a young man, also waving.

As they shot past, Chadwick struck him a glancing blow on the jaw. Red's head struck against the window frame. Chadwick seized the wheel again.

"Stop it! Both of you!" Flowers cried. "Someone throw the switch!"

They passed a sputtering flare. Red saw the sign with the blue ziggurat as he drove his elbow against Chadwick's head, knocking him back into his own seat. His hand shot forward then, flipping the switch back to automatic drive as he began the turn into the exit.

The brakes were immediately seized as Flowers announced, "Roadblock!"

The tires screamed. The land to the left of the road fell away sharply. The slope to the right was more gradual, if rockstrewn, above the yellow earth . . .

Red twisted the wheel to the left. It turned right.

"Sorry, boss," Flowers said. "One of us is wrong, and I hope it's you."

Something soft and heavy enveloped him as they left the road and hit the slope. He heard the door open. He was ejected.

Falling, hitting the ground, rolling . . . He lost consciousness. For how long he could not tell, though it did not seem a great while.

He could hear the crackling of flames. There also

seemed to be some distant shouts. He took several deep breaths. He stretched and relaxed. Nothing seemed to be broken . . .

He began struggling with his cocoon. It was a tough, white, foamy substance.

The shouts came nearer. More than one voice, but he still could not make out what they were saying.

He worked his hands around to his stomach, up toward his chest. There was a sudden pang along the left side of his ribcage.

He caught hold of the fabric before him, scratched at it, dug in with his fingers, drew upon it. Slowly it parted. He adjusted his grip, pulled harder.

It tore open. He spread his arms and pushed downward. It came away from his shoulders. He began to crawl out. He heard Leila's voice calling his name. He saw her running toward him.

He turned away and looked down the slope to where his truck lay on its side, burning. He tried to rise, but his foot caught in the spongy material and he slipped back into a sitting position on the grass, catching himself with his arms. His side still throbbed.

"No," he said as he watched the truck burn. "No . . ."

A hand rested on his shoulder. He did not look up.

"Reyd? . . ."

"No," he repeated.

Below them, the truck suddenly blossomed into a ball of fire. Moments later, a wave of heat arrived. Red raised his left hand just as Randy came up and halted several paces away.

"You could have been in there . . ." Leila began.

His hand shot forward, a finger extended.

The flames fell back. A tower of smoke rose. Something seemed to be moving within it, traveling a slow spiral upward.

"There," he said. Then, "Now I understand."

A huge graygreen dragon-form rose above the smoldering vehicle.

"It was Chadwick whose time had come," she said. "All of your actions were meant to serve him."

Red nodded without taking his eyes from the twisting, drifting shape. All of its movements were graceful, and somehow verged on the erotic. It was an air-dance of freedom, release, abandon.

Abruptly, it halted and looked their way. It spread its wings and drifted toward them. When it was very near, it managed, somehow, to hover.

"Thank you, children," it said, in a voice rich and melodious. "You have done for me that which I did not know to do for myself."

It circled slowly above them.

"What is the secret?" Red asked. "I remembered more than you did. I thought I was arranging things for myself."

It looked upward to where another dark form was now drifting.

"Events, child. Events, and their unconscious manipulation," it replied. "I cannot advise you, for we are all different. Keep looking, if you feel you must. For you, that may be the way. But your time is not yet come. When it does, help may come from anywhere— a friend, an enemy, a stranger, a relative . . . As for me, I am going home now. Let us hope to meet again one day."

It twisted sharply and began to rise in the morning light, its scales gleaming like golden mirrors. It began to move its wings, slowly at first, then faster, climbing, dwindling as they watched. Another winged form passed near it. Soon they were gone from sight.

Red lowered his face into his hands for a moment. The wind had shifted and the smell of his burning vehicle came to him now.

"Will someone please come and pick me up?" came a small voice from down the hillside, "before this god-damned vegetation takes fire?"

"Flowers?" he said, dropping his hands and beginning to rise.

But the young man was there before him. He retrieved the book, encased in an ejection pod, and carried it back up the hillside. Red stared at him.

"Reyd, I'd like you to meet your son Randy," Leila said.

Red frowned.

"Where you from, boy?"

"Cleveland, C Twenty."

"I'll be damned . . . Blake—or Carthage?"

"Yeah. But I'm using Dorakeen now."

Red stepped forward and took Randy by the shoulders, looked into his eyes.

"I'd say so, I'd really say so, and you're welcome to it. What are you doing here?"

"Looking for you. Leaves showed me the way. Then I met Leila—"

"I hate to break this up," Leila said, "but we'd better move that car up there before someone else comes along."

"Yes."

They turned back toward the feeder road.

"Uh— What should I call you? Father?"

"Red. Just Red." He looked at Leila. "My head is suddenly clear. Something like a fog seems to have gone."

"That was the last dark bird," she replied.

"You know, I'd have missed Randy here, if that had been me."

"Yes."

"Let's go to Ur for a beer. They always have good beer in Ur."

"Okay with me," Randy said. "There are a lot of things I want to ask you."

"Sure. There are plenty of things I want to ask you— and we have plans to make."

"Plans?"

"Yes. The way I see it, the Greeks still have to win at Marathon."

"They did."

"What?"

"That's what the history books say."

"You got on at C Twenty. Where?"

"Near Akron."

"Can you retrace your route?"

"I think so."

"We're going to do it! Wait! We'll stop at Marathon first, to check the scorecard. Some new factor may have come into play."

"Red?"

"Yes?"

"I don't know what you're talking about."

"That's all right. I'll explain—"

"Mondamay will be looking for me," Flowers interrupted. "I think you'd better leave a message."

Red snapped his fingers.

"Right. You guys move the car. I'll be back in a minute."

He turned and jogged back down the slope, holding his side. He picked up a hot, twisted chunk of metal, to scratch HAVING LUNCH IN UR. —RED on the buckled door of his still-burning pickup.

"Does reality always seem a little out of step around him?" Randy asked.

"I never noticed anything strange," said Leila, patting her pockets, shrugging and exhaling a small flame to light her cigar, "until after the other fire. But he seems his normal self again, now."

" 'De ce terrible paysage, tel que jamais mortel n'en vit, ce matin encore l'image, vague et lointaine, me ravit . . .' " Flowers began. "Perhaps I, too, am a dragon —only dreaming I am a book."

"I wouldn't put it past you," said Leila, climbing into the car. "Leaves, meet Flowers."

There came a double burst of static.

Two

In a mountain fastness in C Eleven Abyssinia, Timyin Tin regarded the lovers.

Pressing close beside him, Chantris ran a dark pinion
over the bandaged head and back of the tyrannosaurus.

"Poor dear. That's better now, isn't it?"

The tyrannosaurus moaned softly and leaned against
her.

"Thank you for the use of this delightful bower," she
told Mondamay, who had helped to dig them from
the ruins of Chadwick's palace, "and you, little man,
for assisting us with transportation."

Timyin Tin bowed deeply.

"To be of service to a dragon of Bel'kwinith is almost
too great an honor for this one to bear," he replied.
"I wish you every joy in this place of your liking."

The tyrannosaurus grunted several times. The dragon
laughed and caressed him.

"He's not much on brains," she confided. "But what
a body!"

"I am pleased that you are pleased," said Mondamay.
"We will leave you to your bliss now, for I must seek
along the Road after my own love. This human de-
stroyer has offered to assist me. After that, we will
make pots and grow flowers. Timyin Tin—if you are
ready, come mount my back."

"You might," said Chantris, blowing a small spiral of pale smoke, "check around the last exit to Babylon, near the sign of the blue ziggurat. We dragons have ways of possessing peculiar information."

"I thank you for that," said Mondamay as Timyin Tin climbed onto his back and grasped his shoulders.

They rose into the air, bellows and shrieks of laughter filling the valley below them.

In a dirt-floored adobe building in Ur, Red, Leila and Randy, garbed in native garments, sat drinking the local brew from clay pots. A swarthy, stocky man, similarly clothed, approached.

"Randy?"

They looked up.

"Toba!" Randy said. "I owe you a drink. Sit down. You remember Leila. Do you know my father, Red Dorakeen?"

"Sort of," said Toba, shaking hands. "Your father? My, my!"

"What are you doing in Ur?"

"I'm from these parts originally, and I'm between jobs just now. Thought I'd come back and visit the folks and set up some more work for myself."

He nodded toward the corner, where several burlap sacks leaned against the walls.

"What sort of work?" Red asked, lowering his crock and wiping his mouth.

"Oh, about sixty Cs up the Road I'm an archaeologist. Every now and then I come back to bury a few things. Then I go forward and dig them up again. I've already written the paper on this batch, actually. It's a pretty interesting piece on cultural diffusion. I've got some really nice artifacts from Mohenjo-Daro this time around."

"Isn't that—uh—sort of cheating?" Randy asked.

"What do you mean?"

"Planting things that way— You're messing up the archaeological record."

"Why, no. As I said, I am from here. And they'll really be six thousand years old when I discover them."

"But won't you give people a distorted idea about Ur and Mohenjo-Daro?"

"I don't think so. That guy I was drinking with over in the corner is from Mohenjo-Daro. Met him at the 1939 World's Fair. I've done a lot of business with him since."

"It's a very—peculiar—occupation," Randy observed.

Toba shrugged.

"It's a living," he said. "I'm pleased to see you're still alive, Red."

Red smiled.

"It's an occupation," he said. "As a matter of fact, we were just discussing it . . ."

Somewhere, the Red Baron and Saint-Exupéry were going at it over the French countryside. Joan saw their forms in the sky, like battling crucifixes . . .

A small man braked his black Volkswagen when he saw the blue pickup truck turn over and begin to burn. He watched for a time, then continued on . . .

Alone, important and wise, the great dragons drift above Bel'kwinith, dreaming roadmaps.

The messenger collapsed on the steps of the Acropolis. He delivered the news from Marathon before he died.

About the Author

Roger Zelazny was born in Ohio, began writing at age twelve, holds degrees from Western Reserve and Columbia, has been a professional writer since 1962, is married, and lives in New Mexico with his wife Judy and sons Devin and Trent. He is the author of eighteen novels and four story collections. He is a three-time winner of the Science Fiction Achievement Award ("Hugo"), has received the Science Fiction Writers of America Nebula Award on three occasions, the French Prix Apollo once, and has had one book chosen by the American Library Association as a Best Book for Young Adults. His works have been translated into twelve foreign languages and have been dramatized on stage, screen, and radio.

Roger worked for seven years as a federal civil servant before quitting to write full-time. He is a past secretary-treasurer of the Science Fiction Writers of America. His best-known books are probably *Lord of Light, Doorways in the Sand,* and his five-volume Amber series. He speaks often to campus audiences. He is currently working on a full-length animated film "involving elements of American Indian mythology."